C000006234

LOGISTICS

LOGISTICS

A CHRISTMAS STORY

CHRIS COPPEL

Copyright © 2022 Chris Coppel

The moral right of the author has been asserted.

Apart from any fair dealing for the purposes of research or private study,
or criticism or review, as permitted under the Copyright, Designs and Patents
Act 1988, this publication may only be reproduced, stored or transmitted, in
any form or by any means, with the prior permission in writing of the
publishers, or in the case of reprographic reproduction in accordance with
the terms of licences issued by the Copyright Licensing Agency. Enquiries
concerning reproduction outside those terms should be sent to the publishers.

Matador
9 Priory Business Park,
Wistow Road, Kibworth Beauchamp,
Leicestershire. LE8 0RX
Tel: 0116 279 2299
Email: books@troubador.co.uk
Web: www.troubador.co.uk/matador
Twitter: @matadorbooks

ISBN 978 1803130 170

British Library Cataloguing in Publication Data.
A catalogue record for this book is available from the British Library.

Printed and bound in Great Britain by 4edge Limited
Typeset in 11pt Minion Pro by Troubador Publishing Ltd, Leicester, UK

Matador is an imprint of Troubador Publishing Ltd

To Clare. I couldn't do this without you.

CHAPTER
ONE

1981

Tony Brusco was desperately trying to get a few more minutes of sleep before pandemonium broke out in their tiny Newark apartment. It was Christmas morning and so far the kids were still sleeping. He knew it was only a matter of time before one of them woke, remembered what day it was, then charged into the living room to see what Santa had brought them.

He hoped that it was something decent as the only toys that they could afford to buy them had come from the discount aisle at the local Target. Thankfully, as Mia was only three and Joey was a month shy of five, they hadn't yet got to the stage of wanting branded clothing or electronics. Still, he'd had to almost empty their bank account just to buy them the cheaply made gifts that nobody else seemed to want.

Life hadn't been fair to Tony.

He'd studied hard and always planned to go to college and hopefully become a doctor.

He felt he had things pretty much under control until his girlfriend, Sofia, took him aside one day in the school hallway and told him that she was pregnant with what turned out to be their son, Joey.

"I thought you'd...you know...protected yourself," he replied, stuttering. "You said, it's okay, I got protection."

"No, I didn't. You don't never listen. I said it's okay so long as you have protection."

They married three months before Joey was born and for the next couple of years lived with Sofia's parents.

It was not a great time for anyone.

Sofia's parents blamed Tony for ruining their daughter's life. They had hoped that she would one day be the first person in their family to go to college. Had they bothered to occasionally listen to their daughter, they would have known that she had no intention of spending even one more minute in a classroom after she graduated high school.

When Sofia announced that she was expecting for the second time, things got even worse. Her parents would hardly even look at him. The upside was that it gave them the impetus they needed to start looking for a place of their own. Thankfully, Tony had a regular job at the local Quicky Lube and had managed to save up enough for them to pay the first and last month's rent on a tiny two-bedroom walk-up apartment.

Despite the troubled road that had carried them there, Sofia and Tony were in a good place. They had a roof over their head, two beautiful children and, though they would never openly admit it, were still madly in love.

For Tony, college became just another dream that hadn't quite materialised; despite that, life wasn't really that bad. Money was always tight, but they both knew that things could have been a lot worse.

Tony tried to snuggle Sofia, more for warmth than for anything else, but, just as he moved onto her side of the bed, he heard the sound of little feet scampering down the hall towards the living room. Moments later, the morning's tranquillity was irrevocably shattered as both kids began screaming from the other room.

"He's been here," Joey screamed at the top of his lungs.

"Santa, Santa, Santa," was all Mia could manage in her state of over excitement.

"Time to get up," Sofia mumbled.

"Just gimme a few more seconds, please," Tony begged.

"You know that's not going to happen today, right?" she insisted.

"If I'm getting up, then you have to do the same," he countered.

The two reluctantly got out from under their warm comforter and put on their dressing gowns and slippers.

They walked into the living room with forced smiles and feigned excitement at finding the gifts they'd bought under the tree. Dotted among the ones that they'd stayed up late wrapping the night before were some new ones covered in expensive-looking gift paper and with bows that looked like they cost more than both the Target gifts put together.

Can I open mine?" Joey asked. "Please?"

"You and Mia should open your presents at the same time, so no one feels they're more important," Sofia instructed.

The two children seemed to have a sixth sense about which presents were going to be the best. They moved the gifts from Target off to one side and each grabbed one of the presents that had materialised overnight.

After a few seconds of almost feral ripping of bows and paper, they both squealed with delight. Each had gotten exactly what they'd asked for in their letters to Santa. Joey got the walking robot that shot missiles while its eyes turned bright red, and Mia cuddled the talking teddy bear she'd been dreaming about all year.

Tony and Sofia looked on as the kids then opened their Target presents. Tony pretended to be happy with an off-brand, battery-operated toy train engine, even though a piece of it had already broken off in the box. Mia looked down at her colouring book and pencil set with a mix of disappointment and confusion. The set reeked of cheap and, even at her tender age, she could tell.

While the kids grabbed their Christmas stockings from where Tony had pinned them to the side of the dining table (they had no mantlepiece), Sofia reached under the tree and picked up her present for her husband.

"It's not much, but I saw you looking at it in the store," she said as she handed it to Tony.

He carefully removed the wrapping paper, knowing that Sofia would find some later use for it.

Tony roared with laughter as he opened the box.

"I love it. I really do," he said as he held up his gift so the children could see. It was a bright red Christmas tie with a reindeer on the front. Its red nose protruded from the polyester material.

"Push the button on the back," Sofia said. "I already put the battery in it."

Tony found the concealed button and pressed it. The red nose began flashing. Tony pressed the button again and it flashed even faster.

"I love it," he grinned. "I'm gonna wear this to your parents' house."

Tony tied his present around his bare neck, then did a cheesy male-model pose for the kids.

"Open what I got you," he said, pointing to the back of the tree.

Sofia leaned in and grabbed the box. She was just wondering what he could have bought her that was so light, when the Christmas tree skirting, made of an old white sheet made to look like snow, suddenly moved.

"What the...?" Sofia said, startled. "What have you done, Tony? You know the super don't allow no pets in this building."

Joey and Mia, having heard the exchange, gathered back at the tree to see what Dad had bought for Mom.

As Joey stood, dumbstruck, Sofia pealed back the fake snow and her jaw dropped open.

Mia shrieked in delight and Joey just started giggling.

Tony and Sofia didn't know what to say.

Curled up, and fast asleep under the tree was a young girl who couldn't have been more than two or three years old. The noise of the commotion awoke her. She looked up at the Brusco family, yawned, then smiled.

"Where dada?" she asked as she rubbed her eyes.

"Oh, that's just great," Tony said. "I asked Santa for a new radio and what does he bring us…another mouth to feed."

"I take it that you're not responsible for this?" Sofia said with a chill in her voice. "Cause if this is your way of telling me that you got a kid with someone else, I'm gonna…"

"Whoa! I got nothing to do with this. I ain't never seen this kid in my life."

"I'm calling the police," Sofia said as she reached for her phone.

"Oh yeah," Tony said, shaking his head. "Why do I get the feeling that we're gonna end up being the bad guys, here?"

Tony's instincts were right.

The police arrived with an entourage. The child was whisked away and immediately checked for any bruising; all they found was an unusual birth mark behind one of her ears. The child services officer then placed her, along with Mia and Joey, "somewhere safe".

Despite Tony's pleading that he knew nothing about how the child came to be in their apartment, proceedings for child kidnapping charges ensued. The legal battle to clear themselves and regain custody of Joey and Mia just about destroyed Tony and Sofia's life as well as greatly limiting all future prospects.

CHAPTER
TWO

Present Day

Holly Hillman woke up as she did every day at exactly five-forty-five in the morning. She didn't need an alarm. It was somehow time stamped into her DNA. She hadn't become one of the most powerful women in New York by lounging around in bed all morning.

Before she even got to her feet, she checked her iPad Pro for any overnight emails or texts that needed immediate attention. As CEO of Marshall Whiteman Logistics, she had an executive suite with eleven highly trained assistants to make sure that nothing ever slipped through the cracks. Despite such support, Holly still made sure that she personally stayed on top of all the important projects with which she was involved.

That's why she was where she was.

Running a company that moved 25% of all global commodities around the world was not for the faint of heart or for the gentle of spirit. Holly was as tough as nails. She also ensured that she was always the smartest person in the room; not by surrounding herself with sycophantic head-nodders; rather, Holly made sure to study everything there was to know about each subject before she ever stepped into a meeting.

Newsweek had proclaimed her to be Woman of the Year two years running. *The Washington Post* had dubbed her the "hardest working woman in America."

Holly didn't care what the media thought of her. For that matter, she didn't care what anyone thought of her. She believed that she had been put on this earth to make Marshall Whiteman Logistics the most powerful and successful logistics company on the planet.

Holly had given up any pretence of a social life and concentrated on nothing but the company. She didn't date. She had never married, had no true friends and had no family that she knew of. These were the sacrifices she'd had to make to retain the razor-sharp focus that was needed to steer the hundred-billion-dollar corporation through the uncharted waters of global logistic domination.

She didn't mind the sacrifices one little bit. Holly couldn't even conceive what possible satisfaction, things like friends and family could bring her compared with the euphoric rush that she felt every day when she stepped into her penthouse office.

Holly loved the power.

And, within a matter of a few months, she would be in a position to wield even more of it.

For over two years, Holly had been shepherding the acquisition of their biggest rival. It had been her plan from the start, and she had ensured that every single eventuality was covered so that on December 23rd of that year, Marshall Whiteman Logistics would conclude the purchase of the Ling Chow Group based in Hong Kong. In six months' time, with the acquisition completed, MWL would control over 42% of the world's commodity logistics. The company value would almost double overnight and Holly's bonus would add over $17,000,000 to her already healthy bank account.

Holly was about to close the iPad when a new email dropped into her inbox. It was from Will Myers, the head of the company's legal department. It read:

> *Re: LCG contracts.*
> *We received all the documentation overnight and everything looks good. They signed off on all conditions as agreed but have added one new codicil. I don't feel that it's a big concern but would like to discuss it with you. I am in the office now. Can we meet when you get in?*
> *WM*

Holly wasn't remotely concerned by Will's news. Last-minute additions weren't unusual. What was a little strange was that Will hadn't attached the new codicil so she could read it. That told her that it was something that he didn't feel should be emailed even though their network was more secure than any private or government operation.

Holly carried out her specific and never-varying morning ritual. She did ten minutes of stretching and light yoga, then showered for eight minutes followed by three minutes drying her short black hair. Her make-up regimen took only two minutes. At forty-three, she still looked under thirty and only ever used a minimal amount of lipstick and mascara.

She checked herself in the mirror and looked deeply into her own aqua blue eyes. This momentary examination was as close to intimate self-reflection as Holly was ever going to permit.

She prepared herself exactly one-half cup of Quaker Oats quick oatmeal, scattered some muesli on top, then drizzled honey over that. She added some unsweetened almond milk, then stood at the kitchen counter eating the same breakfast she had consumed every day for the past twenty years.

After two minutes of teeth brushing, she donned one of her twenty identical dark burgundy dresses she had custom made by a designer in Milan. Holly believed, as had Einstein, that wasting brain cells deciding what to eat and what to wear was a pointless time extravagance in one's life, as well as a complete waste of brain cells.

Holly exited her building at six-thirty, as she did six days a week. On the seventh day, she worked from home. Maibo, the building's cherished doorman, knew not to say a word to her. He had worked at Park Towers long enough to know who liked a little morning conversation and who didn't. Ms Hillman definitely fell into the latter category.

She walked past him as if he didn't exist and stepped to the kerb. Mr Maibo, however, knew that, behind the ice-cold exterior, Ms Hillman always rewarded the building staff with the most generous Christmas bonuses of all the other residents.

Her black SUV was waiting as it always was. Her driver, Paolo, knew that he could set his watch by her coming out of her building. He also knew, just like Maibo, that she wouldn't say a word during the drive and expected him to do the same in return. Neither man cared if she spoke or not. They were perfectly happy with the silence and wouldn't have known what say to her anyway.

Holly gave off an air of inapproachability. Whether it was cultivated or it naturally evolved, it was an effective weapon against anyone getting into her personal space. As her driver turned onto 5th Avenue, Holly texted Will that she was three minutes from her office and to please meet her there.

Holly stepped out of the SUV and walked into the Marshall Whiteman Logistics building at 713, 5th Avenue. She used the executive express elevator that only serviced the 92nd and 93rd floors. Nobody else dared get into the same elevator as Holly. They weren't necessarily scared of her; it was just that her aura of aloofness seemed to fill the space without any additional help.

Three minutes from the moment she'd texted Will Myers, Holly walked into her office suite. While most of the building employees didn't start work for at least another hour, her executive team were already hard at work at their desks. Will was waiting by the double doors that led to her private office.

Holly nodded at Charlene, her executive assistant who'd been with her for almost twelve years, then walked into her private office without even acknowledging Will. He wasn't in the least bit fazed. That was how she was. It wasn't a slight or a snub; it was simply that she wasn't built with the gene that promoted non-essential social interaction.

Will followed her in and sat in one of the two guest chairs that faced her desk. Holly's office was large and had an amazing view of the city, yet, despite being able to see all the way to the Statue of Liberty, it had a certain cold sterility about it. There was no comfortable seating area for more casual conversations or meetings. There was no art on the walls that may have permitted a glimpse into her tastes and maybe even personality. Instead, each wall held one large, framed photo of the firm's four biggest logistic centres that were located in Brazil, Germany, Dubai and Mexico.

An austere looking conference table and six chairs were at one end of the room nearest the door. Holly's expensive but charmless desk was at the other end. There was nothing else. No cabinets, no shelving…nothing. She had no need for such trappings.

When she had taken over the CEO position from Marshall Whiteman himself, the first thing she'd done was to have all the art and bookcases removed. The custom wood floor and priceless Middle Eastern handmade rugs had also been replaced with light grey dense pile carpeting so as to cut down on the noise reverberation and the expense of upkeep.

Will handed her a single piece of legal-sized paper.

"It's at the bottom of the page," Will advised. "It's marked simply as the last condition."

Holly read the paragraph, then looked up at Will.

"I'm not sure I understand what they are asking for," Holly stated.

"Cutting out all the legalese, it basically says that, as

they are going to retain 25% of the company, they want to be assured that those in senior leadership positions are in good enough health to be able to carry out their duties and responsibilities for the foreseeable future. You as CEO are one of the twelve names listed."

"Can they even insist on something like this?" she asked. "Is it even legal?"

"It's unusual, I'll say that, but it isn't illegal. An addendum to the codicil that outlines specifically how the information will be used and what will happen to the specimen and report has been uploaded to our shared drive. They do not appear to have any interest in using the data for anything other than to find out if there are any definitive health issues that could come up within the next five or ten years."

"How can this not be illegal?" Holly questioned. "We're getting into HIPAA territory as well as a million other privacy regulations."

"Actually, we're not," Will replied. "They don't want to see any of the details. All they want is a neutral facility to tell them whether, in the case of each listed person, there is a strong physical predisposition to a catastrophic medical condition that could manifest within the next five to ten years."

"So, they want all of us to have a DNA test?"

Will nodded.

"What if we refuse?" Holly asked.

"If we refuse to accept the last condition, we don't have a bilateral contract."

"Is there any way that they could somehow access the data and look for anything other than the specifics outlined in here?"

She tapped the single sheet of paper.

"Not that I can see. The sample would be destroyed, as would the report. They've suggested that one of their medical officers come here to New York and examine the report with a representative of the DNA sequencing lab. They wouldn't take anything back with them other than the knowledge that the senior executives will continue to be healthy, as far as their DNA can show."

"I could get run over by a bus tomorrow," Holly stated.

"Yes you could, but there's no way to pre-screen for that," Will replied.

"Give me an hour," Holly said as she started to re-read the new condition.

CHAPTER
THREE

Holly called Will fifty-eight minutes later.

"I'll accept the condition only so long as they do exactly the same," she stated matter-of-factly. "I want the twelve top-tier executives of Ling Chow to have the same codicil as they are forcing upon us. I would like the same independent DNA lab to handle both our tests and those of the Ling Chow Group executives."

There was a lengthy silence from Will's end.

"Will?" Holly prompted.

"I'm here. Sorry," he replied. "We've never required that before. Is there a specific reason you feel it to be necessary now?"

"Yes. If they are going to force myself and eleven others of my team to undergo something so private and personally invasive, then I want to ensure that they are willing to do exactly the same thing."

"Isn't that just a little bit disingenuous?" Will asked. "It almost sounds as if we're playing tit for tat here."

"We are, and for good reason. The Chinese have become a leading superpower over the last half century by forcing the west into biased trade agreements, most of which seem to have addendums and codicils that are designed to divert the focus away from something that's been covertly manipulated within the main text of the contract. In the time it will take for them to agree to my 'tit for tat' ploy, as you called it, I want you and your team to go back over every single word of the contract. I will bet you that you will find that they have made some sort of minor adjustment somewhere buried in the legalese that slants a little more of the benefits in their favour."

"You really don't trust anyone, do you?" Will answered.

"No, and I don't feel that I should have to remind you that you shouldn't either," she shot back. "Has there been any more pushback from Washington?"

"Just the usual nonsense. I'm more worried about the growing social media attacks on the company over this merger. They're really promoting Ling Chow's distribution centres as being nothing more than slave labour camps."

"Which they're not," she barked. "We've already gone over this a thousand times. Every single employee at the Ling Chow Group gets paid above the local minimum wage."

"There's also the…" Will began.

"…and the children that work at the centres are all above minimum work age," Holly interrupted.

"I know, but when you compare our minimum pay and age regulations, theirs do sound a little barbaric."

"That's crap and you know it," Holly replied. "The governments where LCG has their facilities set the labour laws. Ten dollars a week here may sound like an aberration, but in most areas where LCG is located, that's considered good money. LCG has brought decent-paying work to every one of the areas where they've built one of their logistics centres. We don't hear the locals over there complaining. If LCG pulled out of those areas, the workers would be back on the streets begging for food. Instead, they have a place to sleep, good food and medical support."

"I know the arguments, but, just between you and me, you've seen their distribution centres. You visited every one of them last year. You can't say that they don't look like prison camps."

"They are clean, and every worker lives less than a minute from their job. Plus, they're healthy and they're well fed," Holly replied. "What could anyone possibly find wrong with that?"

"Other than the fact that the workers have to leave their families behind when they move to the centres?" Will suggested.

"They're still better off than they were before LCG hired them," she said, starting to get annoyed with Will's continued dogma. "Will, your priority right now is to vet every word on every page of the contract that was sent back to us. I know that you and your team have already read through them but do it again. This time word by word and number by number. You will find a discrepancy. I promise."

Holly disconnected the call. She opened her laptop and accessed the shared drive. She wanted to study the details in the addendum to LCG's new condition. As she read the twenty-seven-page document, she couldn't help flashing back to that business trip when she'd toured Ling Chow's logistic hubs with their integrated live-in staff facilities. Will hadn't been completely wrong. The places where the workers had to live were pretty bad. With twenty-foot barbed wire-topped concrete security perimeter walls and their suicide-proof building netting, they were something out of an Orwellian horror fantasy, and those were just the buildings they let the team visit.

Each time she tried to focus on the never-ending text, images of the lost faces she'd seen staring down at her from the LCG residential buildings kept floating to the surface. She had to push the memories away. They were depressing, but they were also very much part of modern global manufacturing and distribution. The poor and the uneducated were no longer thought of as individuals. They were fed and clothed and kept healthy when possible, but only so they could perform repetitive, mindless tasks six days a week for ten hours a day. The only reason they didn't work on the seventh day was because medical advisory teams had determined that, by not giving them anything in the way of a break, it could actually harm both their physical and mental health.

Besides, she kept telling herself, the inside of the buildings had been clean, the cafeterias had seemed decent enough and not one worker had complained when she'd asked about their conditions.

Seven hours later, Will appeared at Holly's office door. He looked pale and was visibly shaken. He was holding a plain manila file folder. In it were two single pages copied from the latest draft of the LCG contract. One was from the returned signed copy, the other from the original sent to Hong Kong earlier in the week.

Holly's doors were open, but she was engrossed in reading the revised projections from their South American hub, which had suffered some minor damage due to a close encounter with an illegal forestry burn off that had raged out of control. She didn't notice Will waiting at the doorway.

Charlene finally had to text Holly that Will was waiting to come in.

"You found something, didn't you?" Holly asked as Will took a seat across from her.

"Yeah," he replied. "I am so embarrassed about this; I don't know what to say. I will of course be submitting my resignation later today."

"Let's stop the theatrics, shall we? Just tell me where they hid it."

Will opened the folder and placed a single sheet of paper in front of her.

"It's the highlighted section," he advised.

Holly read the three lines of text, then shook her head.

"Those conniving little…" she said as she leaned back in her chair.

"It was last place we would have ever thought to look," Will answered.

Holly held the page in front of her and read, "Ling Chow Group employees, management and members of the board, upon bilateral agreement to the contract dated August 12, 2022, with an enforcement date of December 23, 2022, will immediately become eligible to join the MWL pension scheme. Ling Chow Group accepts that their employees, management and members of the board will be able to access any and all funds within the pension plan that were vested prior to the purchase of the Ling Chow Group."

Holly slammed the document back onto her desk. "They took out the word 'NOT'. In a 78,000-word contract, they intentionally removed one word which would have given them the ability to become vested in the pre-existing funds within the pension portfolio. That's over fifteen billion dollars." Holly looked up to the heavens. "Did you bring the same page of the original before they doctored it?"

Will retrieved the other sheet of paper from his folder.

Holly read it aloud. "Ling Chow Group accepts that their employees, management and members of the board will NOT be able to access any and all funds within the pension plan that were vested prior to the purchase of the Ling Chow Group."

"What do you want to do about this?" Will asked.

"If we had more time to play around with these clowns, I would suggest that we find some clause that we can doctor to be in our favour. The thing is, we don't have time. Change the wording back to the way it was and send a revised contract for signature by LCG."

"What do you want to say to them?" Will asked.

"Nothing," she answered. "They will see what we've done and know that they were caught out. Don't even point out the modified clause about their having to match the DNA terms. My guess is that they will sign it and have it back here by the end of the week."

Will gathered the two sheets of paper and rose to his feet.

"About my resignation…" Will began.

"There isn't going to be a resignation. If there was, I'd have to let the entire legal team go. Nobody noticed the change."

"Maybe, but I'm the head of the department. I have to take responsibility for this," Will stated.

"Fine. I now deem you responsible," Holly countered. "Now please go away and let me get some work done."

"I can't help feeling that, if anyone else was standing here in front of you, you would have fired them for this."

"We'll never know, will we?" she replied. "Now go away."

Will shrugged then left the office. He was in shock. He would have bet everything he had that Holly would have fired him on the spot. Hell, if he'd been in her shoes, he would have fired the head of the department that almost gave a Chinese company full access to the corporation's pension funds.

Will knew full well why she hadn't let him go, but it was still a miracle that the ice queen of Manhattan had shown even a modicum of compassion. Will shook his head as he remembered back twenty-two years to when the two of them had spent most of that summer either in bed or wishing they were in bed. Holly was already headstrong and determined to make a name for herself, yet, back then, she'd had a gentler, warmer side even though she tried to hide it from most people. He could still remember distinctly the day that she'd learned that she had been selected for the management intern slot at Marshall Whiteman.

They had bought a cheap bottle of champagne to celebrate and had spent most of the evening in each other's arms laughing at everything and nothing.

One week later, the day before she started the new job, she held Will's hands in hers, looked him straight in the eye and told him that she was ending their relationship. Her reasoning was that she had, from that moment on, to focus every molecule of her being on her career and nothing else. There would be no time for luxuries like a personal life and that included him.

Later that day, as he walked home, crestfallen at having just been dumped, he never imagined that he would one day be working for Holly. He had to assume that she too had never considered that they would end up working together. Yet by some strange twist of fate, ten years later, Marshall Whiteman purchased Dynamic Logistics, where he was the assistant director of their legal department. During the negotiation for the buyout, there had been one particular day when Holly, the newly appointed CEO, had appeared at one of the pre-closing purchase meetings.

Will had heard in advance that she would be attending the meeting and had agonised over what to say when he saw her. He needn't have worried. Will ended up seated almost directly across from Holly in the MWL conference room. She glanced at him once, showed no recognition and carried on with the meeting as if he were a complete stranger. When the meeting ended, he had waited outside the conference room hoping to get a word with her when she stepped out. Despite knowing that he should stay as far away from her as possible, Will felt there were still things to say and could only hope that she felt the same way.

When she finally exited the room, she saw Will leaning against the wall. She stopped in front of him.

"You'll be happy to know that I plan to keep you on. I hear good things about your work," she stated, frankly. "The only condition I have is that you conduct yourself professionally at all times and that there will never be mention of, or inference to, our having once been acquainted."

With that, Holly walked off, leaving Will wondering how their summer of passion and shared love could now be coldly compartmentalised into them simply having once been acquainted.

CHAPTER
FOUR

Holly returned to her co-op apartment just after eight o'clock that night. It had been a long day. She had put out dozens of fires as she usually did, yet still had trouble convincing herself that she was doing enough for MWL. That was the biggest problem with Holly's perfectionism: she was always having to reassure herself that she had indeed done all she could at work for the company and its shareholders.

That night, however, she felt a strange emptiness inside. She knew that, as CEO, she couldn't have performed her tasks with better professionalism, skill and even corporate creativity. She couldn't therefore fathom why she felt hollow and incomplete. Those were emotions that she never allowed behind the walls that she had so carefully constructed in her subconscious.

Holly poured herself the permitted small glass of Chardonnay and stood by the floor-to-ceiling windows of her living room and looked out over the city and the East Hudson River beyond. This was her nightly routine as she waited for the delivery of her dinner from La Caprice. She had given them a monthly dinner schedule over five years ago. Every night, her preselected choice was prepared according to her specific instructions and was delivered at eight-thirty pm precisely. It was another way that she'd managed to save her brain from having to make pointless and time-consuming decisions. By creating her monthly meal plan, she knew what she would be having and when she would be having it without having to expend even a moment of contemplation or deliberation.

Holly watched one of the Manhattan dinner cruise boats fight the tide as it headed upriver. The bright lights from the dining salon reflected onto the dark waters of the Hudson. She knew that there would be music playing on board. She had a momentary flashback to the day that Will had, all those years ago, managed to scrounge a pair of tickets for one of the dinner cruises. It had probably been one of the most romantic nights of her life back when such things actually counted for something.

Like her clothes and her dinners, romance was just another mind-consuming action that was better avoided. She watched the cruise boat get smaller as it receded down the river, then, much to her shock and even amazement, she felt her eyes well up as a wave of repressed emotion passed unexpectedly through her.

Holly knew perfectly well what was troubling her that night. It was when Will had said to her that he couldn't help feeling that, if anyone else had been standing there in front of her, she would have fired them. It hadn't fully registered at the time, but his words had somehow found a place to nest in her thoughts. Of course, he was right. She would have fired anyone else right there and then, but the problem was that it wasn't anyone else. It was Will. It was the only man she'd ever loved. The only man she'd ever opened up to. The same man Holly had pushed away so that she could be free from any distractions as she fought her way to the top.

The thing was it was more than simply needing to keep herself focussed on success. Though she rarely would admit it to herself, Holly was terrified of the feelings she'd once felt towards Will. He'd made her feel safe and strangely complete. She'd started to see her life as a shared adventure rather than as an emotionless singularity. Twenty years ago, while lying next to him and watching him sleep, she'd even imagined a time when they would grow old together and be able to remind each other of the miraculous life they'd had as a couple.

Holly hadn't been able to cope with such emotions. They portended a life that was too perfect and too fragile. Maybe it was because of what happened when she'd been a child, but she had no context with which to understand that such things were actually possible.

Holly was an orphan. She had no memory of her parents. She had been placed under the care of child services at the age of two and a half. From there she had lived with a foster family for six months before being adopted by Marsha and David Gelles. They had been decent people and had raised her with strict values. There had been plenty of affection yet, to Holly, it had never seemed completely genuine. Not that she believed that they didn't love her; she was sure they did. It was just that the very act of displaying any strong emotion seemed foreign to them, almost as if such a display of feelings was something to be avoided at all cost.

Marsha and David were born-again Christians and believed every single word of the New and Old Testament Bibles. When it came to what they referred to as "hogwash fantasies" like tooth fairies and Santa Claus, they wouldn't permit such ludicrous fabrications anywhere near Holly's young impressionable mind. Yet every night, just like clockwork, they would read her passages from the Old Testament and dinned into her that everything they were reading was factual and beyond question or reproach.

Holly had grown up without any fantasies. Her childhood mind had been filled with tales of the endless battles one had to fight between the good as laid out by God and his son, versus the bad of almost everything else.

In a universal display of crushing irony, Marsha and David Gelles had died along with nine other parishioners when they had been attempting to burn copies of Salman Rushdie's Satanic Verses *in the furnace of their church. Somehow the flaming books had fallen back out onto the dry wooden floor, caught the tinder alight and burned the building to the ground.*

Holly was sixteen at the time.

She was alone again in the world, and felt confused at not feeling their loss deeply enough. Holly was rehoused with a new family across the river in New Jersey. Dave and Sky were the existential opposite of her late adoptive parents.

They were the closest thing to 1960s West Coast hippies that could be found in the twenty-first century. Their world revolved around love and forgiveness and peace. Their farm property was huge and shared by thirteen other families. There were dozens of children who were left to basically run wild while their parents, both natural and foster, focussed on peace, love and pot.

The result was that Holly found herself in a vibrant and endlessly fun "community", but there was even more of a disconnect between her and her new foster parents than she'd had with Marsha and David. At the farm, fantasies were allowed to run rampant. Nobody there followed any organised religion, other than flitting occasionally to Buddhism when the mood struck them. Holly was overwhelmed with suddenly having a choice from a smorgasbord of opinions and beliefs. She regretted not having had that upbringing when she was younger, when fantasies should and would have played a much bigger part in her life.

The sound of a gentle knocking on her door alerted Holly that her dinner had been placed in the hall and was awaiting her collection. She shook away the reminiscent thoughts and confused memories and opened the door. The smell of linguini with fresh pesto and chilli shrimp rose up and greeted her. The familiar aroma brought her to her senses and made her feel a sense of comfort.

It also reminded her that it was Wednesday.

Three days later, at exactly five forty-five in the morning, Holly checked her email and saw a note from Will. The

LCG contract had been returned fully executed exactly as she'd expected. Will added that his team planned to work all weekend to review the document just in case they'd not followed Holly's script and tried to again "modify" a clause somewhere.

By Sunday night he confirmed that there were no alterations from the last copy sent by Marshall Whiteman Logistics. They'd reached a point in the proceedings when only Holly's signature was needed to fully ratify the contract. Once signed it would start the process during which both parties would complete final due diligence and preparation for what would be a massive exchange of company data from both corporations.

There was also the newly required chore of having to carry out the DNA testing of herself and the other eleven top executives.

By the time Holly arrived at the office on Monday morning, her team had researched the myriad of DNA laboratories nationwide. Holly had made it clear to her team that, even with all the care in the world, there was always the slight possibility of DNA information leaking out. She had tasked them to find a company that still focussed on research rather than ancestry or law enforcement support. She felt than those were the ones they should avoid. Her last caveat was that the chosen lab had to be either privately held or, if not, it couldn't have any government association whatsoever.

The list was surprisingly short.

Only three came close to meeting all of her requirements but each had some degree of government interface. At Holly's instruction, the team had broadened the search beyond the US borders and had found the perfect facility a few miles outside the city of Nuuk, in Greenland. It only studied DNA for the purposes of research and only rarely carried out projects such as the one needed by MWL and LCG. It was privately owned by an Icelandic billionaire who preferred to work in Greenland to avoid what he considered to be the bustling crowds in his own country.

Neither her board nor that of LCG could understand why their executives had to travel all the way to Greenland when samples could be taken at their offices and shipped directly to the lab. Holly had to point out that if both teams travelled there in person the possibility of the samples being tampered with, or even stolen or lost en-route, was eliminated entirely.

There was also the unstated motivation that for some inexplicable reason, Holly felt a strange sense of pleasure that she would be able to visit Greenland. She'd always had a love for the most northern parts of the planet, though had never had the time or patience to visit them.

After convincing both groups of the security benefits of the trip and finally agreeing on a schedule, the MWL execs flew out on 3rd September. LCG had picked the 7th for their excursion.

Holly and the eleven other MWL executives all met at Teterboro airport at eight forty-five. Though having all the senior management travelling together on the same plane was normally not permitted, Holly waived the policy in light of the urgency of the trip and the fact that they were travelling on MWL's own private jet.

Flying time from Teterboro airport to Nuuk was just

under four hours and the plan was to go straight there, have their samples taken, then fly right back the same day. The hope was that all twelve would be home in time for dinner.

CHAPTER
FIVE

The Teterboro weather had other plans for them. The twelve had to sit in the company's G700 jet for over three hours while dense fog that enshrouded the airport kept them grounded. By the time the Gulfstream was cleared to take off, they were almost four hours behind schedule. Holly realised that, with Nuuk being two hours ahead, they wouldn't even land until seven in the evening. She had no doubt that the lab would stay open for them, but, by the time they were driven to the facility and then had their swabs taken, they would be lucky to be back in the air before nine o'clock. If nothing else went wrong, they would get back to Teterboro by eleven. That was only one hour before the airport closed, after which they would have to reroute to a different airport and thus cause minor chaos for their ground transportation.

Holly didn't like that option.

Never one to leave anything to chance, Holly called

Charlene back at the office and told her to find suitable accommodation in Nuuk for her team and the flight crew, just in case something delayed them still further. She didn't want to be stuck in Greenland with nowhere for her and the other executives to stay. Apart from being unthinkably unprofessional, the management officers would make a point of reminding her of the poorly planned trip at every possible opportunity.

Before the G700 even reached cruising altitude, Charlene called back and advised that all twelve of them and the three crew members were booked into the Hans Egede Hotel in the centre of town. It had multiple restaurants and a bar and was by far the best hotel in Greenland.

Holly doubted that they would need to stay the night but was relieved that an emergency option had been found.

The flight was interminably long for Holly. Being the only woman among a jet full of self-important men was enough to bring on a headache. Though she had become used to their constant bravado, she could practically smell the testosterone as the bucks bragged about various deals and battles that they'd waged and won. Holly did as she always did in such situations and kept her nose glued to her laptop so the others wouldn't feel compelled to drag her into their tiresome conversations.

Four hours after take-off, as the luxurious aircraft started its descent towards Nuuk Airport, the tower advised the pilots that they would have to circle due to an unexplained problem with Nuuk's only runway and that it was temporarily closed. It took over an hour before the tower confirmed that the runway was unobstructed, was reopened, and that they were cleared to land.

By the time they touched down, the entire town appeared to know that they were running so late that they wouldn't be able to return that night and would therefore be staying in Nuuk. It was a rare occasion when even one executive from a Fortune 400 company stayed the night in Nuuk. To have twelve of them at one time was an event worthy of celebration.

The customs and immigration officer who boarded the plane immediately upon landing advised them that a VIP dinner was going to be held in their honour at the same hotel where they were staying. While the execs seemed delighted at the idea of a party being thrown just for them, Holly cringed at the thought of having to go through the social niceties that would doubtless be required of her long into the evening.

Having been cleared for entry, they alighted from the aircraft and were faced with an extraordinary sight. Lining one entire side of the fenced runway were what appeared to be thousands of reindeer, all staring through the fencing at Holly and her team.

A representative from the Proseq DNA lab met the new arrivals on the tarmac. Anna Selguort looked like a model for Nordic cross-country skiing. As she was introducing herself to the executives, she couldn't help but stare across the runway at the giant herd of deer snorting and pushing against the fencing.

"I presume that this isn't that unusual for Nuuk," Holly suggested.

Anna could only shrug. She didn't feel that it was her position to tell the VIPs from Manhattan that she had never in her life seen or heard of such a gathering of reindeer so close to the city or the airport.

Anna led the group to a waiting minibus. Once they were all on board they drove out of the small airport compound. They turned left onto Siaqqinneq Road, then after only a few hundred yards turned onto a private, unmarked, paved drive that led up into the foothills.

Fifteen minutes later they arrived at Proseq. The two-storey, modern steel-and-glass building was surrounded on three sides by untouched rocky terrain. Holly couldn't help thinking that it looked like a giant ice cream sandwich jutting out of the hillside. There was no signage or indication of what went on within the building. Strangely, there were no cars visible outside. It wasn't until the minibus rounded one last bend that they could see that the road seemed to dip and vanish under the left wing of the building.

Anna detected the group's surprise.

"For half the year, it is too cold to park in the open air, so they built the road under the facility."

The guests looked out in amazement as the bus started to drive down the under the lab. A very sturdy-looking steel doorway slid open to let them in.

"Am I correct in saying that Mr Hyertol designed the building himself?" Holly asked.

"That is correct. He created the initial drawing and the architectural plans himself," Anna replied proudly. "He was hoping to greet you personally when you got here but was called away for an emergency."

"Nothing serious, I hope," Holly said.

Mr Hyertol is one of Nuuk's few ordained ministers," Anna explained. "As such, he often gets called away at short notice. I don't believe his task tonight was dire, just urgent. He wanted you to know, however, that he will be at tonight's dinner and looks forward to meeting all of you then."

Once inside, the twelve were led to a modern conference room where two young men in white lab coats were waiting. Another man, wearing a black jacket with the Proseq DNA logo discreetly embroidered on the front, seemed to be supervising the process.

The executives were asked to sit at the twelve chairs at the conference table, but to then swing them around, so they were facing out. In an astonishing show of efficiency and professionalism, the man with the logo then asked to see each person's ID together with their specific QR – encoded ID document that had been sent to them in advance.

Once he confirmed that they were who they were supposed to be, the two men in the white lab coats approached, opened a sealed swab for each person, then took a sample from the inside of each cheek. Each swab went into its own individual pre-labelled test tube and was then sealed.

The entire process took less than an hour.

When they were finished, Holly asked Anna if they could have a brief tour of the facility.

Anna gave her a big smile and answered politely, but emphatically, "No. We do not give tours. We pride ourselves on our ability to maintain complete privacy and security. Nobody but employees of the company can move beyond this part of the building."

Holly smiled back.

"I was hoping that you would say exactly that."

The twelve were gently ushered back to the minibus and were driven back the same way they had come. As they drove past the airport, they could see that the reindeer were no longer standing vigil staring at the runway. They were now lining both sides of the road. As they drove past, every single animal seemed fixated upon their minibus and kept their big, long-lashed eyes glued on it until the bus was completely out of their sight.

The minibus continued towards the town and soon the execs saw brightly coloured houses dotted along the gentle hillside. They would have looked identical had it not been for their different, bright colours. All the houses appeared to be roughly the same size, were predominantly square, and had two floors. A steeply pitched roof sat perfectly on top of each one.

Looking at the functionally efficient, but somewhat bland architecture of Nuuk, Holly was becoming concerned about the hotel. She knew only too well how pampered and fussy her cosmopolitan executives could be. The last thing she wanted was for one of her team to upset the locals with disparaging remarks about the hotel lobby.

She needn't have worried. Once in the centre of the city, they pulled up in front of a gleaming, six-storey building that took up an entire block. The hotel manager greeted them as they alighted from the bus and led them into the hotel lobby. It was modern, clean and luxurious in a minimalistic sort of way. At the far end of the lobby, they could see an inviting looking restaurant which was full of well-dressed people that seemed to be having an exceptionally festive time.

"That is the party that the city has arranged for you," the manager advised. "I'm afraid they chose to start without you."

"How did you plan a party with so little notice?" Holly asked. "I only knew we were staying the night a few hours ago."

The manager smiled warmly back at her. "We are always ready to have a party here. Once your pilot advised the tower that they were not departing until the morning, word reached us within minutes."

The executives only had time to check in and quickly freshen up before attending the dinner that was being thrown in their honour. When Holly walked into the dining room, she was stunned by the number of people who'd chosen to attend the function. All the dining tables had been pushed to the sides of the room to make more space. Along one entire wall was a buffet that began with chilled seafood at one end and ended with exquisitely decorated cakes and cookies surrounding a pot of hot melted chocolate for dunking.

The locals seemed to be enjoying themselves. Most of the men were bearded and most of the women seemed strikingly handsome and surprisingly tall. In one corner of the restaurant sat six diminutive and heavily bearded men, all wearing brightly coloured wool hats pulled down low over their heads. They were merrily drinking what she later found out was Kahlua and cream. They were obviously drunk and were having a whale of a time. One of the group noticed Holly watching them and whispered to the other five. They all then raised their glasses and toasted her from across the room.

One of the strangest sights of the evening was a pair of majestic reindeer that, together with their handlers, were mingling with the guests. Each animal had a dark-red velvet blanket over its back with the logo for a renowned Danish whisky emblazoned on it. On top of the blanket was a leather saddle-like contraption. Instead of a place to sit, there were leather cradles suspended from it. Dozens of bottles of Isfjord Single Malt whisky were nestled within the carriers.

A spokesmodel accompanied each reindeer. Their job was to offer shots of the whisky to anyone who wanted it. Many did. As Holly was being introduced to the local dignitaries, a commotion developed somewhere in the crowd. As the town mayor stood on a portable dais and was trying to make himself heard, Holly was suddenly nudged from the back.

She turned and saw that one of the "promotional" reindeer had broken free from their handler and was standing only centimetres away from Holly, staring up into her eyes. People nearby began to laugh until the other reindeer jostled its way through the crowd and also approached Holly. Both animals completely ignored their minders, and ended up leaning on Holly while making gentle mewling sounds.

"They seem to like you," a well-dressed man commented with a smile. "My name is Gunnar Hyertol. I'm sorry I wasn't able to greet you at the laboratory."

Gunnar was a delicate man. He was shorter than Holly and had a shaved head and a precisely groomed goatee. When he spoke, his English was perfect and almost completely free of any accent.

Holly tried to hold out her hand to shake Gunnar's, but one of the deer nuzzled it instead.

"Is this normal in Greenland?" Holly asked as she tried to maintain some degree of poise and professionalism.

"Not even remotely," Gunnar replied, amused. "In fact, I've never seen anything quite like it before. Are you wearing some sort of unusual musk or pheromone-based perfume?"

Before she could answer, Gunnar leaned over one of the reindeer and sniffed her neck. Holly was so shocked at having her space invaded in such a manner that she let out an involuntary gasp. Both reindeer immediately took up a defensive posture, snorting and stamping a front hoof.

"You only smell of soap," Gunnar advised as he took a step away from the two animals.

The two reindeer minders reached their charges and, after some degree of resistance, were able to manoeuvre the animals out of the restaurant. Once they were gone, there was hearty applause, followed by a raucous round of laughter.

The executives from Marshall Whiteman Logistics were wined and dined until the early hours of the morning. By the time Holly finally felt that she could say her thanks and sneak out of the party without offending anyone, it was well past two am. As she walked through the hotel lobby she noticed a strange greenish light flickering and gently pulsating beyond the hotel's front windows.

Holly stepped outside and was immediately hit by the sub-zero winds. She wanted to run back into the warmth of the hotel but was rivetted by the surreal event that was taking place up in the night sky. She knew all about the aurora borealis. She'd seen videos and even a documentary about it. What she wasn't prepared for was the effect that the northern lights would have on her.

Holly started to cry.

She had no idea why. She didn't feel sadness of any kind. In fact, if anything, she was feeling perfectly content and in good spirits.

It suddenly dawned on her that what she was feeling was an overwhelming sense of happiness and belonging. She had no memory of ever having felt that way in her life.

Holly's tears turned into sobs.

CHAPTER
SIX

Holly never had any trouble sleeping.

She kept her mind free of anxiety or stress by staying on top of every situation, thereby removing the main cause of sleepless nights. Holly also prided herself on rarely dreaming or at least rarely being aware of having dreamed anything.

On her one night in Greenland, Holly dreamed a lot. It was the same vision and it kept forcing its way back into her subconscious every time she dozed back to sleep.

She was a child. A young child. She was in an unfamiliar living room surrounded by people she didn't know. There was something strange about the room. Though it was clearly indoors, she felt that she was, at the same time, in a forest surrounded by trees that gave off an eerie flickering light.

The other people in the room seemed angry that she was

there. One man kept pointing and shouting at a group of uniformed men that he'd never seen the child before.

Holly's iPhone woke her at five forty-five. With the late night and the heavy food and alcohol, she wasn't sure she could trust her built-in clock and had set the alarm. Her head felt groggy and thick, and she was shocked when she realised that she actually had a hangover.

Holly never got hangovers because she never, ever drank to excess. She tried to work out why she would have done so the previous night when a cloudy memory fought its way up to the surface.

Soon after the incident with the reindeer, Gunnar had introduced Holly to the group of men she had observed earlier knocking back Kahlua like it was going out of fashion. They all stood to meet her, and she was surprised to see that none of them even came up to her waist. Gunnar explained that they were all part of the same family and were on leave from the factory where they worked, about an hour from Nuuk.

They were a friendly bunch and seemed fascinated to learn everything they could about Holly and her company. Holly asked them why they wore their hats indoors and all six on them gave her a high-pitched titter as they winked at one another. At some point, one of the men had insisted that she join them in drinking a shot of Black Death. Gunnar explained that it was a favourite party beverage in Iceland and had recently migrated to Nuuk. He warned her to be careful. It was lethal.

After much taunting, she agreed to one shot. She downed the contents of the shot glass in one. The clear liquid practically blew the back of her head off. It tasted like a thick, strong potato vodka but with the added flavour of caraway seeds.

Holly vaguely remembered being coaxed into a second one, but that's all she could remember. She also had a cloudy recollection of standing outside the hotel and crying about something, but she felt that was probably just another dream she'd had.

Holly went into the bathroom and took a long shower, then spent extra time brushing her teeth to try and get rid of the taste of caraway seeds and fermented spud.

The flight back to New York was uneventful. Holly tried to get the other executives motivated enough to discuss their impressions of Greenland, but they all seemed shocked at her trying to engage them in a non-business-related conversation, or, for that matter, any conversation. The other problem was that most of them appeared to be suffering from the same sort of malady that she was pretending she didn't have. If she had to guess, she'd probably pick the Scandinavian whisky as being the likely culprit.

Once they landed and Holly was being driven back across the iconic George Washington Bridge, she could see the skyline of central Manhattan off to the right. Usually, the sight of the towering buildings that had been built on a foundation of greed and success gave her a feeling of awe. That day, she saw them in a different light, and could imagine how breathtakingly beautiful the landscape must have been before the city was built.

"It's a strange view, when you think of it, isn't it?" she commented.

Paulo was so shocked that Holly had actually spoken to him that he found himself unable to respond and replied simply with a nod.

Holly had no idea where that thought about the view had come from. She'd never once in her life considered Manhattan to be anything but awe inspiring.

As they turned onto 5th Avenue, Holly was shocked to see hundreds of people blocking the front entrance to the Marshall Whiteman Logistics building. Most were carrying placards. All were shouting in unison.

"YOU CAN'T BUY LCG, UNTIL THEY SET THEIR PEOPLE FREE."

Even in the cocoon-like luxury of the Lincoln, Holly could clearly hear every word.

She couldn't believe that the protesters were focussing their attention on her company. They didn't seem to understand that Marshall Whiteman Logistics were the good guys. They made sure that America and the rest of the world actually received all that crap that they ordered online, and, without MWL, everyone would have to actually go outside and shop in person like they used to. After the pandemic, nobody wanted that to be their only option. MWL employed over two million people globally and most of those were working in countries where an unspeakable percentage of the population were unemployed.

Holly honestly believed that MWL should be given a medal, not have their building surrounded by a bunch of left-wing activists.

Holly grabbed her phone.

"I'm almost in the building," she barked. "Isn't there something we can do about these rioters?"

"They're hardly rioting," Will replied calmly. "Besides, we have a bigger problem than a few protesters."

"I'll be coming in through the alley entrance. Meet me there." Holly disconnected the call.

Paolo turned down a side alley before reaching the picketers and pulled up at an unmarked delivery entrance. Before she even reached the inconspicuous door, it opened, and Will gave her an understanding nod as he held it so she could slip in without being seen by the mob.

"So, what's this bigger problem?" she asked as they walked along a drab utilitarian corridor.

"Remember our friend Senator Amos Welsh?" Will asked.

"Of course, I do. We're his favourite target for criticism whenever there's an election coming up in his state."

"It's almost as if he holds a grudge against you for closing the Arkansas facility," Will said with a trace of sarcasm.

"The place was untenable," Holly snapped back. "The union and the pensions alone guaranteed that we could never make a profit from that hub."

"Moving it to Mexico was certainly a bold move," Will replied with thinly veiled sarcasm.

"Don't start with me today. I'm not in the mood. All I had to eat last night was cold fish washed down with potato vodka."

"Actually, that sounds pretty good." Will grinned.

"Go back to what you were saying about Senator Welsh," she growled. "What's he up to this time?"

"He's called a Senate hearing to review the purchase of LCG."

"You have got to be kidding me." Holly stopped walking.

"And you've been subpoenaed to appear next Tuesday," he advised while taking a subconscious step away from her.

Holly slowly turned to face him.

"And you tell me this now?" she shouted. "You should have called me the moment you heard. I could have been reached in Greenland or on the jet. This isn't good enough. I expect more from you, Will. I really do."

Holly turned and stormed off down the bleak hallway. "When did you receive the subpoena?" she called back without turning around.

"Ten minutes ago," he called after her.

Holly kept walking.

She knew she should say something to Will considering that he'd done exactly what he was supposed to do and that her outburst had been entirely uncalled for, but apologies just weren't part of her business arsenal. She assumed he knew that and would just shake off her earlier outburst.

She assumed wrong.

Will stopped and watched her retreating back. That had been the first time that Holly had actually raised her voice to him. Though he was a lawyer and was used to tempers and displays of aggression, he was not used to such treatment from her. Her reaction had hurt. He didn't know how much more of her dismissive treatment he could take.

Will had recently been giving some thought to dusting off his resume and looking for another job somewhere that didn't involve seeing Holly on an almost daily basis.

Though she clearly didn't seem to hold any residual feelings from their relationship, he did, and working closely with her was pure torture. When MWL bought Dynamic Logistics and Will had joined the company's legal team, he had thought that, by being close to Holly again, some part of what they'd had together would find its way back to the surface and they could maybe even start over, if not, at least be friends again.

All these years later and he was still working there, yet Holly seemed to have erased all memories and feelings towards him. Their interactions were professional, efficient and productive but nothing else.

Will hadn't even wanted to practise corporate law. His father, a federal judge, had made that choice for him.

Will had grown up loving anything on TV or in movies that showed lawyers doing battle in a courtroom. His father believed that his infatuation was because of the pride he felt at him being related to a judge. Nothing could have been further from the truth. Will simply loved the way that opposing counsels engaged each other with cunning and creative logic.

By the time Will was sixteen, his father started grooming him to follow in his footsteps. A summer internship at Whitstable and Koch, Harvard Law, a senior partnership with one of the top ten law firms in New York, then an appointment to the bench.

The problem was that by the time Will was old enough to start following his father's roadmap, he had lost some of the wide-eyed fascination with criminal law. Especially on the defence side, where his father had made a name for himself. He just couldn't find any pleasure in the thought of his spending the next twenty years finding ways of getting guilty clients off the hook. He couldn't see why the system was structured in such a way that the heroes, the poor lawyers tasked with prosecuting the accused, were usually paid a tenth of what defence lawyers raked in. It was no wonder that the greedier lawyers went for the bigger payoffs.

Will spent two summers interning at Whitstable and Koch and, by the end of his second stint, knew that he wanted nothing to do with that type of firm. Their focus was on ensuring that every lawyer billed every second of their time, whether warranted or not, and strategising how to stretch the law to near breaking point, so as to get their client's charges dropped. Will hardly ever saw anyone practising what he considered to be real law.

He needed to find the law he'd seen on TV, where lawyers worked to help clients fight against injustice and inequality instead of spending their time lining their pockets so they could buy a house in the Hamptons and a private jet.

Will decided that he wanted to help people more than he wanted to become rich. On his eighteenth birthday, he sat his father down and told him that he no longer wanted to specialise in criminal law. He felt that he couldn't work within such an unfairly balanced system.

His father initially dismissed Will's opinions, then explained that there wasn't any part of law that didn't favour the wealthy and that he'd better get over that naïve sentiment or he'd end up penniless, living in a cardboard box under a bridge somewhere.

"Fine," Will stated. "Then I won't study law at all. I'll go for an MBA and work for a charitable organisation."

His father stopped laughing. He realised that his son was being completely serious. The last thing he wanted to do was force him to give up law altogether. He still believed that at some point, Will would drift back to criminal law once he'd spent some time practising a different specialisation and came to understand how the whole system really worked.

"I'll tell you what," his father said. "If you are that keen on helping people and feel that criminal law isn't right for you, how about trying business law? From there you could focus on charitable law or even go for that MBA if you really want to."

"I don't know," Will said, shaking his head. "That sounds just as cutthroat as criminal law."

"Not at all. One area is devoted to small business. You could become a champion for struggling shop owners who are being pushed out by wealthy developers. That sounds right up your alley."

Will let his father's suggestion sink in. He knew that he was being played, yet his father's words did make some real sense.

"That may not be such a bad idea," Will said, nodding.

His father watched him walk out of room then smiled.

Will did attend Harvard and did specialise in business law. He was on track, at least in his mind, to focus on small business as his father had suggested when his life took a sharp and unexpected turn.

While window shopping outside Macy's, a young woman walked right into him as she was trying to find something in one of the many shopping bags she was carrying.

That distracted woman was Holly Hillman, and that day was the beginning of their relationship. It was also the beginning of his listening to Holly sing the praises of the corporate world and everything it stood for. Within a matter of months, she had persuaded him to not waste his time focussing on litigation for small businesses.

"Go for the Fortune 400 companies," she insisted. "If you get a job with one of those companies, you can really change the world."

As Will leaned against the cold, breezeblock wall, he knew that the time had come. Feeling no kinship from Holly was bad enough. The fact that the new version of Holly seemed to have lost all traces of the compassionate young woman he used to know, and now her having no respect for him whatsoever, was simply too much.

Way too much.

Will decided that would stay until the Ling Chow purchase had been completed, at which point he would work somewhere a little gentler where there was at least some trace of caring and compassion. Maybe he could even go back to his original plan of helping small businesses.

Just the thought of getting away from the corporate environment, with its relentless need to do nothing but make money, made him feel relaxed for the first time in months.

CHAPTER
SEVEN

In the days leading up to the hearing, Will tried on numerous occasions to meet with Holly to prep her for the Senate inquisition as well as come up with some shared strategies on how to reply to or deflect the negative comments that would come from the junior senator. He knew that he would be able to offer suggestions at the actual hearing but was also very aware of how much Holly liked advance preparation.

Holly never responded to his calls or emails. Finally, on Saturday morning, Holly called him and advised him that he wouldn't be joining her at the hearing, and that she had already structured what she felt would be a winning strategy.

It wasn't the first time that he'd seen her act on her own gut feeling rather than confer with legal counsel. It was, however, the first time she'd blown him off for something so important and potentially impactful as being grilled by the United States Senate.

The witch hunt, as Holly referred to it, was being held in the main Senate hearing room. She had no doubt that it was chosen for its size so that Senator Welsh could make certain that there were as many members of the media in the room as possible. The good senator from Arkansas used the Senate floor and the hearing rooms as his own personal self-promotional TV studios.

Holly entered the hearing room without the expected entourage of legal councillors. Instead, a young boy walked beside her. He was thin and slightly built. His dark hair was slicked back and parted down one side. He was dressed in what appeared to be brand-new khaki trousers, a blue blazer and a light blue shirt that contrasted with his dark skin. The room went eerily quiet. Nobody had any idea of what Holly had in store for the committee. Especially something that would involve a child.

Holly and the boy were seated facing the daunting, semi-circular row of senators.

"Thank you for coming here today," Senator Welsh said from the dais.

"I wasn't aware that I had a choice, Senator," Holly replied bluntly.

A murmur ran through the attending audience.

"I would like to start by—" Welsh began.

"Before you kick off your little publicity show, I would like to introduce Tran Mi," Holly interrupted. "Tran is sixteen and has worked at Ling Chow's Cambodian facility for over eighteen months. I would like to yield the floor and ask for your permission for the room to hear what Tran Mi has to say before we go any further."

The members of the media that were wedged between

the senators and Holly all moved a fraction closer to the boy so as not to miss a word. They knew, as did everyone else in the room, that things looked as if they were about to get interesting for a change.

Senator Welsh was taken aback by Holly's surprise request and was about to deny Holly her motion until he saw that every camera in the room was pointed straight at him. His politician's reptilian brain rapidly calculated the reaction to what many might perceive as a slight, possibly even a racial one, to the young boy.

"Mr Li has two minutes," Welsh declared. "Does he need a translator?"

"My name is Mi not Li, and why are you asking Ms Hillman that question?" Tran replied to the senator in a heavily accented, but strong voice.

The hearing room erupted in laughter. Welsh had to bang his gavel numerous times before the chamber had again quietened.

"You have the floor," Welsh stated bluntly. "You may sit if you wish."

"I could not do that in such a place of high honour. If you would please permit me, I will remain standing."

"As you wish." Welsh sat back in his high-backed, leather chair.

All attention was on the boy. He looked down at Holly as if waiting for her approval to proceed. She smiled and nodded. Tran seemed to stand just a little taller as he faced the senators.

"I am here today because I have heard that you do not agree with the way the Ling Chow Group treats their workers. I felt that someone like myself needed to come here and explain some things to you. You don't know our culture, our needs or what it means to be employed in our country. Yet you feel comfortable labelling a work system that exists 9,000 miles away to be inhumane and oppressive."

Tran took a deep breath before continuing.

"When I was twelve, my father was killed when he stepped on a landmine that had been made, planted and then abandoned in our soil by Americans in the 1960s. That left our family with only the income from my brother and what my mother could make at a clothing factory that supplied T-shirts to many large American brands. We got by until this very committee decided that the factory where she had worked her entire life was inhumane. You ordered the US companies to immediately move their business to a manufacturer in Vietnam. A factory that by strange coincidence donated generously to a super PAC that helped get you elected, Senator Welsh."

There was a murmured gasp from the media and audience.

"My mother's factory was forced to close a few months later because of the lack of customers. We were left to struggle with only the one income from my brother, who worked in another factory that manufactured the very same American souvenir flags that are sold right here in the Senate gift shop. Han, my brother, is paid three cents for each flag he makes. I noticed that you sell them for fifteen dollars. I am not sure how humane that is."

Tran paused to let that sink in.

"There was no way that we could have survived on Han's salary, so I applied for work at the Ling Chow facility fifty miles from our home. Thousands applied, but I was extraordinarily lucky and was chosen. I had just turned fifteen, which is the legal working age in Cambodia. I was transported at LCG's cost to the facility. I was trained and given a place to sleep, medical care, free food and was paid enough to send more money home than my mother and brother together had ever earned. Yes, the hours are long, and yes, I can only visit home once every sixty days, but I am able to support my family and even save a small amount for an emergency. I count myself as one of the lucky people in my country."

Tran let his eyes pass across the dais, making sure to meet the stare of every senator.

"That is my story," Tran stated in a strong and proud voice. "I would now like to know why you feel that you should have a say as to whether I work or not. It is, as far as I can see, none of your business. If you were able to close every factory in eastern Asia that doesn't adhere to American standards, you would put close to a billion people out of work. I am but a peasant boy who knows nothing of the complexities that you must have to deal with every day. You are tasked with keeping your country safe. You must ensure that your people have food and medicine. It is in your hands whether global initiatives find their way into the world's history. There is no doubt that you all have an awesome responsibility. Therefore, please explain to me why you are here today, seemingly for the sole reason of ensuring that I, like millions of others in my country, will no longer have a place to work and be able to support my family. Thank you," Tran finished. He bowed at the senators, then sat down.

The audience and the media started to clap. Slowly at first, but within seconds they were all on their feet, clapping and cheering.

Senator Welsh brought down his gavel to silence the room, but the crowd stayed on their feet and, if anything, applauded and cheered even louder. He was about to bring his little wooden hammer down even harder when the senior senator from Illinois, who happened to be the chairman of the committee, took Welsh's arm and gently shook his head.

Welsh was about to argue when Senator McCleary whispered in his ear. "Not today, Amos," the venerable politician said. "There ain't no way to get the genie back in this bottle. Let it go."

Welsh stared at McCleary as if he were crazy. "Some little kid from a rice paddy in the middle of nowhere isn't going to come into my hearing and stop the wheels of justice!" Welsh declared.

McCleary patted him on the shoulder. "I'm afraid that that's exactly what that boy just did. Now shut this circus down, or I will," McCleary said as he covered his microphone with the palm of his hand.

Three hours later, Holly walked back into her office suite in New York.

"We all watched it on CSPAN," Charlene said. "It's about time someone put that horrible senator in his place. It's even more satisfying to actually watch it happen, live."

"I didn't do anything," Holly replied. "Tran was the star today."

Charlene nodded her agreement. "What a brave and proud young man."

"He certainly was."

"Will wanted to speak with you when you returned," Charlene said.

"Tell him I'm free now," Holly said as she walked into her office.

A few minutes later Will knocked.

"Come in," Holly said as she finished reading a financial analysis for the company's East Asian operations.

"That was some performance today," he stated.

"You sound concerned," Holly commented.

"I am. I wish you'd gone through legal before bringing what in America would be considered a minor halfway round the world to speak on the company's behalf in front of the Senate and the world."

"It worked didn't it?" she replied distractedly as she continued reading the report.

"That's not in question. You used the boy as a strategic prop and, yes, it worked amazingly well. I don't suppose that you got formal permission from his mother in Cambodia?"

"Nope."

"I also assume that Tran didn't have a passport, so I hate to even imagine what laws you broke to get him past US immigration," Will continued.

Holly leaned back in her chair, stared up at Will and gave him a frustrated look. She pressed a button under the right side of her desk and the double office doors automatically closed behind him.

"Sit down for a minute." She gestured to a chair.

She waited for him to be seated before continuing.

"Has Tran left the country yet?" Will asked before Holly got a chance to talk.

"There is no Tran. Michael Sok, however, is back at Georgetown University, where he is studying advanced economics for his master's degree."

"At sixteen?" Will blurted out.

"First of all, Michael is twenty-two and, before you ask, yes, his parents knew all about it," Holly advised. "Michael is the son of the CFO of the Ling Chow Group."

"Why didn't you tell me?" Will asked.

"I didn't tell anyone at MWL. I felt that, as I was about to basically commit perjury in front of a Senate hearing, I should involve as few people as possible."

"But that boy is attending university only three miles from the Capitol. Someone's going to recognise him."

"No, they won't," she stated. "He was in make-up for ninety minutes in a van parked on the Mall before making his appearance. You will be happy to learn that he looks nothing like the Tran Mi that testified today."

"Was it worth it?" Will asked solemnly. "Lying to a Senate hearing just so that workers in Asia can continue being mistreated?"

"Completely," Holly shot back. "Senator Welsh is finally off our backs and I doubt that he will be permitted to do much more harassing of our business practices. The senate leadership knows full well that any attempts by him to continue poking into our affairs will reach the media, who in turn will run the tape of Tran's speech and report that Welsh is being intentionally vindictive. They've had enough bad optics over the last few years. They're not going to let one member create an entirely new media circus."

Holly could see that Will was pained.

"What? I just helped ensure that the sale would go through."

"But at what cost?" Will replied. "Welsh isn't wrong about the conditions in some of those hubs. They've basically got children working as slaves."

"I'm not going to have the same argument with you. The children are better off with employment than without. That's a fact."

"Do you honestly believe that?" Will leaned forward and looked directly into her eyes. "Don't give me the CEO answer. I want to hear the Holly answer from before she joined Marshall Whiteman."

"There is no Holly from before MWL. Whoever and whatever I was back then is gone. Do you honestly think that I could have got to where I am today if I had been weighed down by all those ludicrous 'do-gooder' ideals that are so in vogue at the moment?"

"No. You absolutely wouldn't have gotten to where you are now. But would that really be such a bad thing?"

"Yes. It would be a terrible thing. It would have been a waste of my life and my talents," Holly replied. "I am now in a position to literally change the world. That means a lot to me and it should to you as well."

"But are you changing the world? I'm not talking about making obscene profits for Marshall Whiteman, I'm talking about making changes that matter."

"Profit does matter," she insisted.

Will got to his feet.

"All I can say is that the old Holly would care about changing the lives of all those children in East Asia for the better. Not in sweeping their misery under a carpet of lies and greed."

Will turned and walked out of the office.

Holly watched him as he reached the closed doors and stop. She hesitated in activating the mechanism to open them. His words had hit a nerve. She felt that she needed to say more to him, but at the same time didn't want to lower her emotional barriers.

They had taken too long to build.

She reached under her desk and pushed the door release button.

CHAPTER
EIGHT

Four days after the LCG executive visited the Proseq lab to have their samples taken. Gunnar Hyertol, the CEO of Proseq, called Holly.

"Mr Hyertol," Holly answered. "I wasn't expecting to hear from you so soon. I thought you required twelve days to fully sequence the samples."

"Good morning, and please call me Gunnar. The time frame is still the same; however, we have detected an anomaly with one of the samples from your group."

"That's a nuisance," she said as she calculated what that could do to the purchase schedule. "May I ask which sample was defective?"

"I didn't say the sample was defective," Gunnar explained. "It's the result that has provided anomalous data."

"Doesn't that mean there had to be something wrong with the sample?" Holly asked.

"We won't know that until we obtain a new one and are able to view the results."

"What exactly was wrong with the result?"

"As part of the testing sequence that you requested, we ensure that we are able to find a familial match to the DNA donor's place of origin," Gunnar explained.

"I don't remember asking for that data," Holly voiced.

"When looking for a predisposition to a serious medical condition, we have to take into account the origin and history of the donor's gene nucleus. The location of its origin can ultimately have a bearing on the DNA's gene expression and chromosomal development."

"You've taken me far beyond my knowledge comfort zone," Holly advised.

"That's why you chose Proseq for this project, if I'm not mistaken," Gunnar replied. "We are experts in what we do and hope that our clients trust us enough to leave the science to the scientists."

Holly hated not being on a level playing field when it came to knowledge, but reluctantly understood that she could not develop PhD – level knowledge of DNA and the sequencing protocols from one night of online study.

"Fair point," she acquiesced. "Please go on."

"The sample in question produced a negative 99.999% familial result."

"99.999%! That's good, isn't it?" Holly asked.

"What that means is that there was NO familiar DNA marker for 99.999% of all known global familial traits. It's therefore impossible to trace the location of the genome origin," Gunnar advised. "That is not a good thing."

"How is that even possible?"

"I have never personally encountered such a finding, but, as we often discover, anything is possible. It just means that the donor came from somewhere from which we have no DNA data."

"Where could that even be?" Holly asked.

Gunnar laughed. "That's the rub. That .001% doesn't show as existing in our databases. It could be from a tribe deep in the Amazon basin that has never been tested. It could be a group of nomads that exist in some Himalayan valley. We just don't know."

"That remote?" she gasped. "So, which one of my team turns out to be related to Bigfoot?" Holly asked.

"I'm afraid it's you, Ms Hillman," Gunnar advised. "I wouldn't worry, though; it's almost certainly a problem with the sample we took. Normally I would suggest that I have one of our staff visit you in New York to take another swab, but I know how concerned you are about the security for the testing and the samples."

"I'll fly there tomorrow," Holly announced. "I have a morning meeting I can't miss, but, if I take off by eleven, I'll be with you just after five o'clock your time. Is that agreeable?"

"Of course it is. Will you be flying straight back?"

Holly opened her mouth to say yes, that she would be returning the same day, but instead replied, "No. I'll fly back the following morning."

She disconnected the call and tried to work out why she'd suddenly felt the need to say that she'd go all the way back to Greenland. Someone from Proseq retesting her in New York would have been fine considering the issue at hand. Even more disturbing was why she had said that she would stay over in Nuuk. She most certainly had better things to do than spend another night that far away from her work.

As Holly texted Charlene to book the plane, hotel and a helicopter to get her to the airport, she suddenly tasted caraway seeds. At the same time, the memory of the northern lights swept over her and she immediately felt her eyes begin to tear.

"Good grief!" she exclaimed as she reached for the unused box of tissues she kept in her desk drawer.

Later that night, as she stood looking down on the city and awaited her food delivery, she suddenly began reflecting on her childhood. She had no idea why. Holly made it a point to never look back. There was no good reason to watch a rerun of one's past life. It was the future that counted. Still, try as she may, she couldn't seem to stop her mind flipping open pages that she really didn't want to see.

CHAPTER
NINE

Holly's first memories were cluttered and confused. All she had was a vague vision of being loved by parents that she couldn't even picture. Even as a young child, she'd felt a level of safety and security that she'd never had the luxury of feeling ever since.

Her first short but vivid memory was of waking up under a tree and having strangers yelling both at her and at each other. She had no idea where she was or where her parents had gone. She had never in her life woken up in the morning without hearing her father singing and her mother kissing her awake on the forehead.

People in uniform tried to calm the situation, but to little avail. Holly could remember being put in the back on a strange car and being taken to a place where the sound of screaming babies intermingled with the smell of overfilled nappies. She had snippets of indistinct mental images of living in that strange, unfriendly place until, one day, a couple of people she hadn't seen before whisked her away and took her into their home and their lives.

Unlike the previous place, her new home was spotlessly clean and always, very, very quiet. Holly, even from a very young age, had to learn how to live by the old saying, of her being seen but not heard. The couple took good care of her and treated her well. There was little in the way of affection but, even at three years old, she could tell that they meant her no harm and would do what they could to keep her safe.

As Holly grew up in the quiet house she became used to the routines that had to be strictly followed. Every morning, all three of them knelt in front of a portrait on a bearded man in a white robe and, with their eyes closed, praised his life and the goodness that he brought to the world. It was years before Holly knew who he was and what their words actually meant. Each day when the man left the house, the woman would clean it from top to bottom until mid-afternoon, when she, together with Holly, would sit only inches from a television and watch a man in a blue suit alternate between shouting and crying before finally telling his viewers that the only way to avoid damnation was to dig still deeper into their pockets so that his humble church could continue spreading the message. At least once a week, the woman would suddenly grab her purse, reach for the phone and give her details to a caring and loving operator so that the poor preacher could have the funds he needed to keep the money pouring into his mega church, so that his inspiring words could find their way into people's homes.

Holly distinctly remembered starting school and could recall some of the other kids looking at her with unbridled curiosity. It wasn't until years later that she learned that her home-cut hair and bland, overly modest clothing was not the norm. The other thing that came as a complete shock was that, when Holly tried to bring up the subject of Jesus Christ, our lord, the other kids didn't know who she was talking about or weren't that interested.

As the years passed, Holly came to realise that her home life was unlike anyone else's. In the early days, when the inevitable happened and the first kids started to tease her, Holly just laughed at them and explained that they wouldn't find it so funny when she was taken up to heaven and they were cast down into hell.

Her words upset so many children that two things happened almost simultaneously. All teasing stopped and the school and the principal had a meeting with Holly and the man and woman who took care of her (it wasn't until she was thirteen that she began to accept the fact that they were to be considered her parents).

The principal explained that the school accepted all recognised religious beliefs, and admired Holly's attempts to teach the word of God within the school. However, they could not permit her threatening fellow students with eternal damnation whenever any of them disagreed with her.

Holly had to promise to not wage any further religious campaigns on school grounds. Though her parents seemed to agree while sitting in front of the principal, once they were in the car driving home they covered her with praise and admiration.

Holly managed to refrain from foisting her beliefs on others and did her best to fit in. Thankfully, by her fifteenth year, the thought of boys was dominating most of her thoughts. Despite her rigid religious indoctrination at home, once she stepped foot on the grounds of Lodi High in New Jersey, her thoughts strayed far from the good book. In a strange act of serendipity, her newfound interest in the opposite sex had the unexpected benefit of helping her fit in with some of the other girls in school.

Now that her words weren't trying to spread peace and goodwill throughout the school, and instead were focussed on which guy looked the cutest that particular day, she was welcomed into many of the lunchtime cliques.

By her sixteenth year, Holly was actually enjoying school. Her favourite class was economics, which normally would have lost her some brownie points, but, since she used some of her knowledge to show her friends how to best budget and manage their allowances and savings, she averted the stigma.

On a particularly fine spring day, Mr Berristone was explaining depreciation and how to use the CAP rate. She was furiously taking notes when the principal knocked, then entered the classroom. She scanned the twenty-five faces until she focussed directly on Holly.

"Holly, would you mind coming with me, please?"

Mrs Mudgepince (or fudge pants as she was known among the students) sounded sombre and anxious, neither of which were in her usual vocal repertoire. Holly followed her into the hall and walked silently behind her all the way to the principal's office. Standing in the darkened room were a uniformed police officer and a short, fidgety woman with bright orange hair. She reminded Holly of a baby orangutan.

Her first thought was that she had done something wrong, though for the life of her she couldn't think of one single indiscretion. Holly was even more baffled when fudge pants left the room, shutting the door behind her.

The woman stepped towards her and took Holly's sweaty hands in hers.

"I have some terrible news for you."

The funeral for her parents couldn't be held at their regular church as that had been burned to ground after their failed attempt at exorcising the evils of one particular best-selling book. Instead, the service was held at the Lodi Cemetery and Cremation Centre. The chapel they were assigned was small, which was probably a good thing as there were only twelve mourners. Most of their friends had either died with them in the church fire or had been seriously injured.

Half of the attendees were dressed in gloomy clothing, perfectly suited to the occasion. The other half seemed as if they were wearing the only formal-ish clothing they owned. Holly wondered who they were until a woman in her forties, wearing no make-up, a dark purple muumuu and leather sandals rose to her feet and walked up to the pulpit.

It turned out that she was the sister of Holly's recently departed semi-mother. Her name was Sky and she gave an impassioned speech about how she hadn't spoken to her sister in twenty years, yet their bond had remained strong. Holly wondered just how strong the bond could have been considering that, in the thirteen years she'd lived with her, her semi-mother had never mentioned her sister once. The woman, along with about half the congregation, wept openly as the two caskets were wheeled out of the chapel through a curtained rear door.

Holly was surprised to find that she was not one of the ones crying. She felt sad, obviously, but not to the point of tears. They had certainly stepped in when her real parents abandoned her, but she'd never felt any great love towards them. She wasn't even sure if they would have wanted such personal affection anyway.

As Holly watched the twin pine boxes leave the room, she knew what was next in store for them. She had been stunned when she learned that they had chosen cremation. Holly wondered if the irony of burning them into ash when only a few weeks before they died by the same process, was only obvious to her. She shook away the inappropriate thought and watched as the few mourners began filtering out of the chapel.

Holly became fixated on wondering who the others were who had accompanied her step aunt (by adoption) to the service.

She found out minutes after the service ended. As she walked out of the subdued light and into glaring sunshine, she had to close her eyes for a moment to adjust to the drastic change.

"I know how you feel, poor girl," the woman from the podium stated.

Holly pried her eyes open and saw that she was surrounded by the entire group.

"I hope you don't mind, but I wanted to introduce myself to you the moment I saw you," Sky announced. "I only found out two days ago that Marsha had passed. It was also the first time I'd heard of you."

Holly had no idea how to respond to the statement so simply nodded.

"I know that your poor head must be filled with questions. Where will I live? What will become of me?"

Holly was struck with the strange realisation that she hadn't been thinking those things at all. She started worrying *whether, despite all the teachings of goodness and humility, Marsha's words had fallen on deaf ears and that she was not a good girl at all.*

"You will be happy to know, that I have already been in touch with social services and as your mother's (adoptive mother, Holly thought to herself) only living relative, they were only too pleased to grant me and my life partner, Dane Daniels, full guardianship.

Holly looked at the woman with a confused expression. She had no idea what a guardian was, but she doubted that it could have much to do with her.

"That means you're coming to live with us," Sky explained. "Isn't that wonderful?"

"When?" Holly asked, not fully able to process what the woman was telling her.

"That's the best part. You will be dropped off tomorrow at your old home so that you can decide what to take with you, then you get to come with us."

Sky saw that the girl was still not completely understanding what was happening, otherwise she would have been almost certainly dancing with joy.

"First," Sky said as she gestured for the others to get closer, "let me introduce you to a few members of the household. First, this lovely angel is Spirit. She's my eldest and is hoping to get a place at UC San Diego, next year."

Spirit was indeed waif-like. The single gardenia pinned in her hair, plus the silver peace sign pendant that lay just above her ample, suntanned cleavage, told a story, in and of itself. Her piercing blue eyes locked onto Holly's. "Hi," she said in a gentle, zen-like voice. "We're going to be best friends forever."

As the rest of the group were being introduced, Holly understood at that moment that her life was about to radically change.

As it happened, there was little that Holly wanted to take away from her old house. She hadn't had much to call her own anyway, but what there was didn't need to be part of her new life. She took one last look around the living room, then walked out of the Lodi house for the last time.

Holly climbed into the VW and was whisked away to Glen Ridge, New Jersey. Though she was still in the same state geographically, it felt like a different planet. The farm where she would live until her eighteenth birthday (and beyond that, if she so chose) was about two miles outside the town, nestled between a stream on one side and forested land on the other.

Sky and her partner, Dane, had said little for most of the drive, but, as they wound their way up their unpaved drive, they pointed out various things of interest to Holly. There was the bridge of peace, which may once have looked drab, having been built from the local stone, but was now painted in every colour imaginable. Next they passed what had once been a barn but was now, according to her guides, the group meeting house. It was painted bright purple and atop its canted roof was a single small flagpole, from which flew the striped colours of the gay pride flag.

Holly had never heard of gay pride, let alone their flag, but once she'd met Dane who looked a few years younger than Iris, had long black hair, light brown complexion and was very much a woman, the pieces began to fall into place.

"Is all this property yours?" Holly asked.

Dane laughed. "Not exactly. There are fourteen families and we each own a share of the property."

"Do you all live in the same house?" Holly asked, concerned.

"No," Sky jumped in. "There are three families who share the main house, but the others have their own homes on the property."

As Holly tried to get her head around this surprising revelation, Dane pointed to a large A-frame house a few hundred yards down a smaller dirt track.

"That's where we live."

When they were within a few hundred feet of the house, Dane honked the horn. Three children came bounding out of the front door. Moments later a statuesque woman in her late twenties stood in the doorway and waved.

The children were Lake, a six-year-old blonde girl, Hope, a twelve-year-old African American girl with straightened red hair, and Maui, a sixteen-year-old boy who looked as if he'd been plucked off the pages of a surfing magazine. The woman at the door was called Stream and greeted Iris and River with a gentle kiss on the lips.

Holly had initially assumed that she was a babysitter, considering that she was too old to be their child, but there was something about the kiss that made her question her assumption.

Life in the commune caused Holly to question just about everything she took for granted regarding home life and relationships. Having come from a home with little passion and no freedom of thought, life with her new family couldn't have been more different. She learned that the area where they lived was filled with similar communes where everyone basically "did their thing" and lived their lives to the fullest.

Holly assumed that she would end up going to a similar school to Lodi High. Because of the sheer number of hippy-like families in the area, the school she was to attend had been built specifically to cater to them. The parents did not want their children taught histories of war or slanted opinions about the planet and its origins. Instead, they were taught with an honest purity that most schools had lost trying to follow political correctness and a curriculum that seemed to change with each administration. When Holly saw the brightly dressed kids pile out of the buses, she had a worrying thought that these children were not going to be as bright as those she was used to sitting with in class. She couldn't have been more wrong. The children were sharp, inquisitive and respectful of the teachers and school administration. It was as if they all understood the benefit of getting a good education.

Once the teachers got an idea of Holly's knowledge, interests and learning capacity, they began quietly moulding her in preparation to be able to get into whatever university she wanted to attend. The hippy school, with its "outdated," open learning policy, had a college acceptance rate that hovered around the 93% mark.

Once Holly turned seventeen, the faculty and staff included her in their plans and suggested that NYU was almost certainly the best fit for her. There was no doubt that Holly was destined for a career in business and NYU had the best undergrad and MBA course on the East Coast. As she moved into the twelfth grade, something clicked inside her. She had always been good at school, but, with the knowledge that she was being groomed for the big leagues, she threw herself into her studies like someone possessed.

The bizarre dichotomy of her self-imposed rigid study routine and the easy-going lifestyle of her current home were not lost on her. While the other children her age were discovering the joys of sexual experimentation alongside the heavenly raptures of the commune's home-grown weed, she was buried in books on economics and business administration.

Other than one awkward and clumsy make-out session with her surfer-dude and unrelated brother, she kept her focus on the prize.

It was worth the sacrifice. Her SAT scores were record-breaking and she was offered a full ride, including accommodation and meals at NYU in central Manhattan.

Despite her belief that she had not formed any serious long-term bonds with her hippy family, she found herself in tears as they dropped her off outside Goddard Hall, right next to Washington Park in New York.

To no one's surprise, least of all hers, Holly excelled at the university. Despite her attempts at remain aloof from the partying and field trips, she was still subject to peer pressure over the fact that she didn't seem to be interested in boys, or girls for that matter. She explained to anyone who would listen that she had her whole life to do that. At the moment, everything was about getting that MBA so she could get a spot in one of the Fortune 400 companies.

Holly stayed true to her quest throughout her undergrad and graduate time at NYU. It wasn't until she met a cute guy outside Macy's, after graduating with full honours only a few weeks earlier, that she let down her guard and gave herself to Will.

CHAPTER
TEN

The air-limo helicopter picked Holly up the following morning from the MWL roof, and eight minutes later eased to the ground at Teterboro airport, only a few feet from the waiting G700 jet. There were no weather delays or potential runway incursions at the Nuuk airport, so she managed to arrive in Nuuk fifteen minutes earlier than expected.

Anna Selguort was waiting on the tarmac. Instead of the minibus, she had used her own electric I3S BMW. Holly noticed that the woman looked even more like a Nordic model. Especially in the white puffer jacket with the fur-rimmed hood.

"No reindeer today?" Holly asked.

"I'm afraid not," Anna replied. "I can try to get you some if you'd like?"

"That won't be necessary," Holly laughed, assuming she'd been joking, although with her constant business-like expression, it was hard to tell.

"Thank you for coming all this way," Gunnar said as he greeted her in the reception area.

He led her to his private office, which looked out over a rocky shoreline that ended in a rough, grey sea. The room was modestly furnished for function rather than effect. Holly noticed that there were no personal items dotted around the room. No certificates, photos...nothing. It was almost as if Gunnar wanted to keep his office emotionally sterile.

"I've been very worried about those results," Holly stated. "What if there wasn't a mistake? What If I really don't have any origins? I don't know whether I told you or not, but I am an orphan. Could that mean something?"

Gunnar gave her a sympathetic look as he gestured for her to sit down.

"Unless you believe in immaculate conception, you did have parents, and they in turn would have had parents. All that result would mean, if it does turn out to be accurate, is that you come from a very small gene pool. A little like royal families."

Holly simply stared back at him.

"That part was a joke," Gunnar said, smiling. "Let me just get your sample so that Anna can drive you to the hotel and you can relax. I would normally have asked you to be my guest for dinner tonight but one of our biggest investors is in town and wants to meet with me."

"I completely understand." she smiled. "Don't worry about me. I actually prefer eating alone."

"What a sad statement," Gunnar said.

"Why is that sad if it's what I prefer?" Holly asked.

"It's the fact that you prefer solitude to company that makes it sad. At least to me."

Gunnar retrieved a sealed plastic bag and tore it open. Inside was a sterile plastic tube containing two swab sticks. He donned a pair of black nitrile gloves, then stepped over to Holly.

"Open, please," he asked formally.

She opened her mouth and stood stock still as Gunnar swabbed first her right cheek, then her left. He placed the swabs in the tube and replaced the circular lid. He then sealed the samples back into the bag and resealed the top.

"All done," he announced.

"Thank you."

"If I may suggest…on the top floor of your hotel is the Skyline bar," Gunnar advised. "It can be a magical place with views over the town, the Malene mountains and the Fjord of Nuuk. Just stay away from the Black Death liqueur this time."

"You don't have to remind me," Holly smiled. "You'll let me know as soon as you have the results?"

"You will know the results almost immediately after myself."

"Almost?"

"I am a scientist, Holly. In life just as in my work, there are always unexpected variables."

Before Holly could comment on Gunnar's obtuse comment, Anna stepped into his office.

"Ready to go?" she asked.

"I guess I am," Holly replied with a trace of sarcasm.

As Anna drove out from the underground parking area Holly saw that it had started to snow.

"It's a bit early for snow, isn't it?" she asked.

"Not remotely. Our summer consists basically of July and August. For the rest of the year, snow can always be expected."

"Don't you find that a little depressing?" Holly pressed.

"Not at all. I love snow," Anna replied. "I think it's fair to assume that everyone who lives here likes snow to some degree, otherwise I'm pretty sure they would choose somewhere else to call home."

They drove on in silence.

"What if they had to stay here?"

"Nobody has to do anything that they don't want to do," Anna stated.

Before Holly could continue her interrogation, Anna pulled up under the portico of the Hans Egede Hotel. The same manager from the previous trip checked Holly in and offered her the same room.

As Holly walked towards the elevator lobby, a well-dressed man and a woman stepped in front of her. Something about the pair made Holly feel that were selling something.

"Sorry," Holly said with a smile before either of them could speak. "Not interested."

Holly then sidestepped the pair and snuck into a waiting elevator.

"But..." was all the man could say before the doors slid closed.

The first thing Holly noticed when she stepped into room 217 was a beautiful holly plant in a decorative pot sitting on the writing desk. A note was taped to the base. It read simply: Welcome Back.

Holly smiled at the gesture but at the same time wondered who it was from. She also felt a slight sense of annoyance as she wondered how she was going to lug the thing all the way back to New York, or at least as far as the jet. She did not allow plants or pets within her home. They required care and commitment. She wasn't willing to take on either of those responsibilities.

Holly dropped off her overnight bag, freshened up, and was about to settle down with her laptop when she suddenly decided that she wanted to give the Skyline bar a try. She took the elevator to the fifth floor and followed the signs.

CHAPTER
ELEVEN

It was nothing like she imagined. For some misguided reason, she thought it would be a twee, local watering hole that had tried but failed to look even remotely cosmopolitan. The Skyline bar turned out to be something quite special. The views that Gunnar had promised were spectacular. The room itself was modern, had a great vibe and was beautifully furnished in earth tones and dark wood. The bar took up most up one wall and was lit from overhead by moody purple lighting.

It was too early for the live music to have started, which was fine with Holly.

"Welcome to the Skyline bar, Miss Hillman. What can I get you?"

The bartender was young and clearly had Inuit genes somewhere in his family tree.

"How do you know my name?" Holly asked.

"Mr Hyertol called and said that a beautiful American

woman would be visiting tonight and that I was to take good care of her."

"What's your name?" Holly smiled.

"Minik," he replied.

"What does that mean?" Holly sat on one of the barstools.

"It's a type of natural oil used to waterproof traditional hide boats," he stated matter-of-factly.

"How odd," she said before she could stop herself.

"Not at all. It was an essential ingredient to the lives of my elders."

"I didn't mean to…" she began.

"Don't worry about it," Minik interrupted. "It is a strange thing to call your son, but you'd be surprised how many Miniks there are in Greenland."

He gave her an engaging smile.

"What are you drinking?"

"I'll have a glass of Chardonnay if you have it," she answered.

"Of course we do," Minik replied as he turned to the glass-fronted fridges behind him. "Do you prefer oaky or buttery?"

"You know what? I changed my mind. May I have a large Kahlua and cream instead?"

"Drinking like a local, huh?"

"When in Rome," Holly replied, while wondering why the heck she'd just changed her order. She only ever drank wine, and, even then, in moderation.

As Minik prepared her drink, the same well-dressed couple from the lobby who had tried to sell her something entered the bar. Despite the place being almost empty, they chose to take the two bar stools right next to Holly.

Minik placed Holly's Kahlua and cream in front of her, then turned to the newcomers.

"Donna, Blit, I heard you were in town. Welcome," Minik greeted them. "The usual?"

"Yes please, Minik," Donna replied.

The woman's accent was most unusual, and Holly couldn't place it. Holly glanced casually to her side to get a better look at the couple. Up close, there was something very different about them. They had an exotic vibe as though international travel was a daily occurrence. As with most wealthy people, it was hard for Holly to guess their age. They were both tanned and neither seemed to have a single visible wrinkle. Between the scalpel and Botox, that wasn't unusual anymore, but Holly somehow didn't think the pair had been altered. They were simply healthy and quite obviously highly pampered. She knew that her earlier appraisal of the pair about their wanting to sell her something was completely unfounded.

She tried to get a read on their clothing, hoping that would give some her idea of their country of residence, but she didn't recognise the style at all. The clothes were expensive-looking and immaculately tailored but didn't seem to quite fit any fashion style that she was aware of.

"Holly, may I introduce Blit Zen and Donna Eir? They also work in logistics, as you do," Minik said. "Donna and Blit, this is Holly Hillman from New York."

"Would I know your company?" Holly probed.

"I greatly doubt it," Donna replied.

"Try me," Holly insisted. "I like to think that I know all the competition."

"We are called Eina Nótt Global," Donna advised as she studied Holly's face to see if anything registered.

"I apologise. You were right. I actually haven't heard of you," she admitted.

"You wouldn't have. We have but one client and consider ourselves to be very much a boutique operation."

Minik delivered the couple their drinks in two frosty pint mugs. The liquid within appeared brown and cloudy.

"What are those?" Holly asked.

"Oat mash ale," Blit replied as he took a long swig of his drink.

"I've never heard of that before," Holly commented.

Minik removed a shot glass from the shelf, then filled it from an unlabelled draught tap. He placed it in front of her.

"It's not to everyone's taste," he advised.

Holly sipped it. She had never tasted anything like it. Its flavour was something between oatmeal, hay and grass. It wasn't what she was expecting at all. To make matters worse, it was served slightly warm, which somehow made the taste even more repulsive.

She placed the unfinished shot glass back onto the bar.

"What do you think?" Blit asked with a huge grin plastered on his smooth face.

"I don't wish to be rude, but that was really horrible," she declared. "It must be an acquired taste."

"Not for us." Donna beamed. "They start us on the stuff when we're being weened."

Holly stared at the pair in shock. "They gave you alcohol when you were still babies?"

"It's not alcoholic," Minik advised.

"That's a relief, though if there's no booze in it, and it tastes like it does, I really can't see the point."

"That's because you're not—"

"Why don't the three of you sit over by the window," Minik suggested, interrupting Donna. "Mr Hyertol had me reserve that centre table for you."

"That's a great idea," Blit said as he slid off the stool. "That gives us a chance to talk more about the logistics and distribution business."

Holly normally would have run barefoot over hot coals to avoid having to sit with strangers who were obviously part of a far smaller business operation than she was used to.

She opened her mouth to decline the offer of leaving her place at the bar, but instead replied, "That sounds like a wonderful idea."

"May I get you another Kahlua?" Minik asked.

Holly started to say yes but instead something completely different came out.

"Do you have any Black Death?" she asked. "I had it in the hotel last time I was here."

"I'll bring it your table," he said with a knowing smile.

As the three made their way across the bar, Holly was desperately trying to work out why she seemed to be losing control of her speech. She would think one thing then say something completely different.

Minik brought a small carafe nestled on a bed of crushed ice. Next to that was a single shot glass.

"May we have two more glasses, please?" Holly asked.

"Not for us," Blit declared. "We never drink alcohol before we're going to fly."

"I know what you mean," Holly said. "Even one glass of wine on a plane and I immediately get sleepy. "Does that mean you're leaving tonight?"

"Hopefully in a few hours," Blit began.

Holly poured her first shot and downed it in one. She trembled once, then involuntarily smiled.

"Then again, that depends on you," Blit finished.

"Why does you flying tonight depend on me?" Holly asked, confused.

"Have another drink first, then I'll explain," Blit suggested.

Holly had no intention of drinking another drop until she'd heard what they were up to. She was about to demand that Blit explain himself when, instead, she poured herself a shot and drank it. She looked at the empty glass in wonder, then shrugged and poured another one.

"I'm ready," she announced in a slightly slurred voice after knocking back her third Black Death.

"Yes," Blit agreed. "I think you are. The fact is, we are here specifically to speak with you."

"Whatever for?" Holly asked, surprised.

"We're here on behalf of our employer," Blit stated.

"He believes that you may possibly be his daughter," Donna added.

Holly, who was never short on words, couldn't respond. She just stared at the pair with her mouth agape.

"I believe that Mr Hyertol advised you earlier that your DNA results were highly unusual," Blit said. "That the origin of your family could not be matched with anyone or anywhere on record."

"Go on," Holly slurred.

"Our employer believes that you may well be his long-lost child." Dona explained. "He lives an incredibly unique existence, and his family location has been kept a secret for a long time."

"Let me guess." Holly rolled her eyes. "He lives somewhere where nobody has ever given their DNA."

"Our employer, was the only member of his family who has done that," Blit replied. "And that was only so that his DNA could one day be matched, and he would finally be able to find…you."

"What I want to know," Holly said, wagging her finger at Blit, "is how the heck did your employer ever hear about my DNA? It's supposed to be a big secret."

"It is a secret," Donna said. "to everyone but our employer."

"Proseq guaranteed security and anonymity," Holly announced. "I could sue them for this."

"You could, but I fear that you would lose," Donna replied.

"The thing is that your father…" Blit began.

"Potential father," Holly corrected him.

"Your potential father is the only real client of Proseq and is also the backer for the entire operation," Blit explained.

"He created the lab for the sole purpose of keeping track of global DNA records," Donna added. "He hoped that, one day, someone would have the exact genomic markers that yours did."

"How long has your boss's daughter been missing?" Holly asked.

"Just over forty years," Donna replied. "She went missing in 1981."

Holly drank another shot of Black Death.

"That's funny," she nodded. "That's when I was found abandoned."

Donna and Blit shot each other a knowing look.

"Would you like to meet our employer?" Donna asked. "We have a car downstairs."

Holly theatrically waved for Minik to come to the table.

"You seem to be enjoying the drinks," Minik commented once he reached the table and saw that the carafe was empty.

"These two people want to take me for a drive...hic," Holly said as she tried to focus her eyes. "Do you vouch for them or should I be concerned that they have nefar... naffeer...nefarious plans for me?"

"I give you my word that these two wonderful beings will take exceptionally good care of you," Minik replied.

"Okay...if you say so," Holly replied as she unsteadily got to her feet.

The others stood by and had their hands at the ready in case Holly had any trouble with her balance.

"Whoa," Holly giggled. "Must be the altitude or something."

Minik again glanced down at the empty carafe. "That must be it," he concurred.

Blit and Donna helped Holly through the hotel, then out onto the portico. A bright red Range Rover was parked directly in front of the building. The vehicle's paint didn't just shine; it gave off a warm, lustrous radiance that seemed to actually glow in the dark. From the headlights all the way to the taillights, there was a single delicate gold pinstripe that appeared to almost twinkle.

"What a pretty car," Holly exclaimed.

"We like it," Blit replied. "Why don't you get in the back? You'll be more comfortable there."

He opened the rear door for her. Holly looked cautiously inside and was stunned to see that, instead of expensive leather seating, the seats were covered in fur throws. Little twinkle lights were strung across the back window, giving the interior a warm comforting light.

"That better not be real fur," Holly scolded.

"It hasn't been for a long time," Donna replied.

Holly ducked inside and snuggled into the layers of faux fur.

"Wow. This is so comfy," Holly sighed.

"There's a warm coat to your left," Donna stated. "I suggest you put it on."

Holly couldn't see the point but did as she was told and slipped on a heavy-duty black puffer jacket.

"I'm going to bake in this thing," she commented.

Blit and Donna gave each other a knowing glance before climbing into the front seats.

Holly noticed a woven basket against the back of the driver's seat. She removed a red and green gingham cloth and saw a chilled glass of milk and two chocolate chip cookies.

"Are these for me?" she asked.

"Yes," Donna responded. "You'll want those when you wake up."

"What do you mean wake up?" Holly asked. "I wasn't planning on going…"

Holly suddenly smelled a wonderful mix of peppermint, chocolate, vanilla and cloves.

"My favourites," she sighed as she fell into a deep sleep.

CHAPTER
TWELVE

Holly dreamed of glorious things. There were break-dancing swans, ice-skating penguins, possums performing a synchronised water ballet and even a pair of orangutans in top hats and tails dancing to Irving Berlin's *Puttin' on the Ritz*.

At one point she felt the interior of the car get much colder and she had to wrap some of the furs more tightly around herself.

She was just starting a new dream about flying through clouds of meringue and whipped cream when the car went over what seemed like a big bump and woke her up. She stared sleepily up at the roof and marvelled at the way they'd painted an authentic looking night sky together with stars and a bright new moon.

Something about the painting was wrong. She reached up to touch it and found that there was no roof. It took Holly a few moments to realise that she was looking up at the actual night sky. She sat bolt upright and looked around the rest of the interior.

She saw that it was completely different from when she'd first climbed in. There was no roof or even windows. There weren't even any front seats.

That revelation suddenly hit home.

Where the front seats and driver should have been, there was nothing except a wooden dashboard that curled outward. Holly then noticed that there wasn't even a front to the car anymore. It was gone. In its place were two reindeer in full harness that appeared to be pulling what was left of the vehicle. It was then that all the pieces fell into place.

It was a sleigh. She knew then that she had to still be dreaming. It was a great relief and, instead of feeling the panic that had started to rise within her, she felt she could relax and enjoy the ride.

The reindeer on the left then turned its head and looked directly at her.

"We'd hoped you'd stay asleep till we landed," it said. "This has to be a bit of a shock for you."

Holly recognised the voice. It was the man from the bar. It was Blit.

"You'd better hold on tight: we're on final approach now," Blit advised.

Holly tried to calm herself and get her thoughts together. Something was nagging inside her.

"Blit Zen and Donna Eir. Blit Zen and Donna Eir," she kept repeating to herself. "Blit…"

"Everything alright back there?" the other reindeer asked in a voice that sounded exactly like Donna's.

Holly leaned forward and stared at the two animals.

"Donna Eir and Blit Zen?"

She knew she was so close.

"No way," Holly suddenly exclaimed. "Donner and Blitzen!"

Both animals turned back to look at her.

"This would be a good time to eat the cookies and drink the milk," Donner shouted from the front.

"I think she's starting to work it out," Donner said.

"I like her. I hope she's the one," Blitzen replied.

Holly wolfed down the cookies and downed the milk. She immediately felt calmer and strangely content. She collapsed back into the comforting pile of faux furs. Whatever the dream was, she knew she just had to let it play itself out. The ride became choppier. She leaned her head over the side of the sleigh and saw that they were flying over a blanket of white. She also noticed that they were getting closer to it.

By the bluish light of the stars and a slender crescent moon, she was able to see that it was snow. In every direction, and as far as she could see...snow.

There were no buildings or any other signs of habitation, yet the sleigh continued to get closer to the ground.

"Would you mind pressing the button in front of you that says landing lights?" Donner requested.

Holly played along with the dream and looked at the dashboard. Amidst the various instruments, knobs and switches, she saw two buttons. One said OB Landing Light, the other said GND Landing Lights.

"There are two buttons. One for OB one for GND," Holly shouted.

"Might as well push them both," Blitzen called back.

Holly carefully pushed the OB button and, much to her amazement, the sleigh and the harnesses for the reindeer lit up as hundreds of tiny bulbs blinked on.

"Now the other one," Donner called out.

Holly pressed the second button but couldn't immediately see that it had done anything.

"I don't think that one worked," she shouted over the wind noise.

"Look forward and down," Blitzen replied.

Holly shimmied herself to the front of the sleigh and looked between the harnesses and the deer. Off in the distance, she could see two rows of lights. One side was red, the other green. They were parallel to each other and seemed to stretch out for over a mile. Between them and the lights, three illuminated chevrons flashed on and off, pointing them towards the snow-covered runway.

"That's perfect," Donner called out. "You can settle back in the seat now. We're on the glide slope and about to land."

Holly did what she was told and watched as they got closer and closer to the ground. Then, with hardly any bump at all, they were no longer in the air and instead were skimming across the snow as the two reindeer galloped along at full speed.

As Holly looked out for any sign of life, the sleigh began to slow down. It came to a full stop midway along the lit strip, but she still couldn't see anything but snow. Holly, dazed and confused, was about to ask Donner and Blitzen to explain what was going on when the right-hand sleigh door swung open and a man in a dark suit seemed to appear from nowhere.

He was young and immaculately dressed. Holly thought that he looked like a successful Manhattan executive. Strangely, even though it had to be below freezing, and Holly had buried herself under layers of faux fur to stay warm, the man wasn't wearing anything over his suit.

"Holly Hillman?" he asked offering his hand. "I'm Travis Michaels."

"That's me," she replied.

"Let's get you out of the cold," he suggested. "I have some paperwork that needs your signature before we can take this meeting any further."

"Signature on what?" she asked. Even in a dream state, Holly still knew better than to sign anything without her legal department checking it out first.

"It's just a couple of NDAs and a liability waiver."

"You want me to sign a non-disclosure agreement? Why? All I've seen is snow."

Travis took her hand in his and gently coaxed her out of the sleigh. He then led her a few feet away.

"This will feel strange at first, but the sensation goes away almost immediately," Travis advised.

He took one more step and vanished, yet his hand was still visible and was holding tightly onto hers. She stepped forward and was instantly transported into a warm space where Travis was again visible next to her. Even though they were out of the cold, Holly was able to look behind herself and see the sleigh and reindeer where she'd left them moments earlier. It was as if they were behind a thin veil. The area in front of her appeared to be a strange opaque barrier. She thought she could see some shadowing beyond it but couldn't be sure.

"What is this place?" she asked.

"This is what we call a dimensional annex. It's a space between two dimensions. The one you came from and the dimensional rift that we are about to enter. Once you've signed the documents, I can take you the rest of the way through."

"You don't seem to be holding any documents," Holly observed.

Travis laughed. "I think we're ready, Stephanie," he said into the grey nothingness.

A hand passed through from the other side, holding an iPad. Travis took it and the hand vanished. He tapped the screen and retrieved three electronic documents. Travis held the pad out to Holly.

"Each one is a single page. The wording is simple and precise. After you sign one, swipe it to the left and the next one will appear."

Holly reluctantly took the tablet and read the first document. Travis wasn't kidding. The wording was simplistic but all-encompassing. It basically said that Holly agreed to not divulge anything about what she had seen or was about to see while at NPMD.

"NPMD?" she questioned.

"North Pole Manufacturing and Distribution," Travis replied.

"Of course," Holly responded flippantly. "I am still dreaming, aren't I?"

"What do you think?" he answered.

"I think I must be."

"Then there's no harm in signing that you agree not to share what you've seen," Travis said with a smile.

"What if I refuse?"

"We take you back to your hotel."

"What about meeting with this person that claims to be my father?"

"You forfeit that chance," he stated.

Holly considered her options.

"What the heck?" She shrugged.

She signed the first agreement, saw that the second one was an agreement forbidding her from copying any technology she would see on NPMD premises, and signed that as well. She also signed off on the third document, which was simply boilerplate stating that she wouldn't hold NPMD liable for any personal injury while on their property.

Holly handed the iPad back to Travis.

"What now?" she asked.

"Now, I get to change your life."

CHAPTER
THIRTEEN

Travis again took Holly's hand and led her towards the grey barrier through which the iPad and hand had appeared.

"We're not going through there, are we?" Holly asked.

"We have to," Travis replied. "That's where the fun begins."

Holly wasn't remotely reassured by his response. A stranger leading her into a mysterious room while saying that the fun was about to begin sounded like the premise for a low-budget horror movie. She would have resisted if it hadn't been for the expression of excitement on Travis's face and her own overwhelming curiosity.

She closed her eyes and stepped through the barrier at the same time as Travis.

Holly didn't know what to expect, but, if the rest of whatever it was was anything like what she'd so far experienced, it was likely to be mind-bending.

"Are we through?" she asked nervously.

"Yes," Travis replied, laughing. "You can open your eyes now."

Holly slowly raised her eyelids.

She'd never felt such disappointment. They were standing in what looked like the reception area of an industrial factory that didn't need to impress clients. A Formica-topped service desk ran along part of the back wall of a thirty-foot square, drab, utilitarian room. There was a seating area on the right and a flat-screen TV on the opposite wall. Holly was surprised to see that it was playing the movie *Elf* starring Will Ferrell.

"You look troubled," Travis observed.

"I was expecting something different," she replied.

"What exactly?"

"I don't know, but it wasn't this."

"I'm glad to hear that," Travis said as he approached the service desk. The only thing visible on the surface was a metal call bell. He tapped it and a flat chime echoed through the room.

Holly looked on expecting some reaction to the bell. Eventually she heard footsteps approaching. They had a strange sharp clacking sound which reminded her of tap shoes. The door behind the counter opened and the footsteps grew louder, though she still couldn't see anyone. Suddenly the top of a red and green felt hat appeared behind one end of the counter. As it headed towards the centre, it suddenly rose higher, then higher again as the owner walked up on a set of unseen steps.

Holly tried not to stare but found it next to impossible. Standing behind the shabby counter was an elf. A young male elf. Or at least someone dressed as an elf. Holly could only see the top half of him but saw that he was wearing a green tunic with bright silver buttons and a cheery red collar. The longer she stared at him the more she realised that he seemed to be the real deal. He was almost exactly half the size of Travis yet looked to be roughly the same age.

"By the way she's staring at me, I take it I'm her first elf?" the elf asked Travis.

"Yes, you are," he replied. "At least as far as she knows."

"Miss Hillman, I'd like you to meet Harry." Travis did the introductions. "He's been running the service desk for…what is it now, Harry?"

"One hundred and fifty-one earth years," Harry replied proudly.

"Wow!" Holly exclaimed. "That's amazing. How old are you?"

"We don't keep track of how old we are in the rift," he stated.

"Why not?"

"Because we age so slowly, it would be impossible to count." Harry rolled his eyes.

"Miss Hillman hasn't had the briefing yet, so she doesn't understand any of this," Travis advised.

"Oh, okay, that makes sense." Harry nodded.

"What is the 'any of this' that I don't understand?" Holly asked.

"That will come later on when you have your TDO."

Holly gave him a frustrated look.

"Sorry," Travis said. "That stands for temporal dimensionality orientation."

"That sounds like fun," Holly shot back, sarcastically.

"It's actually quite transformative and will give you an understanding of everything that goes on here."

"Here being?" she pressed.

"You'll have to wait for the orientation. I'm not licensed to discuss it."

"Licensed?" Holly shook her head. "Since when does anyone need a licence to tell someone where they are?"

"Sorry," Travis replied. "All I can tell you is that you're not anywhere close to being where you think you are."

"That helps a lot, thanks."

"You sure she's the one?" Harry asked. "She seems awfully cranky to be his daughter."

"Will someone please tell me whose daughter I'm supposed to be?" she pleaded.

"She doesn't know?" Harry blurted out.

"Not yet," Travis replied while giving the elf a dirty look.

"This is getting…" Holly started to say.

A nondescript door next to the TV opened and a female elf stepped into the room. Unlike Harry, the woman wasn't wearing traditional elf garb. Instead, she had on a severe black wool suit, black leather shoes and a grey woollen hat pulled down as far as her ears. She looked older than Harry and seemed highly impatient. She may have only been half Holly's height, but her attitude was definitely full-sized.

She referred to a clipboard she was holding.

"Holly Hillman?" she asked in an officious tone.

"That's me." Holly, for some reason, raised her hand despite being the only visitor in the room.

"My name is Ms Babbitt, and you need to come with me now," she stated.

Holly turned to Travis.

"You're coming, aren't you?" she asked with concern.

Travis shook his head. "I'm only assigned up here in the front office. You need to go with her now.

"But I don't..."

"That's enough lollygagging," Ms Babbitt declared. "We're on a tight schedule if you're to meet the big man today."

She held the door open. Holly looked to Travis, who gave her an encouraging smile and a brief head nod. Holly then took a deep breath and stepped through the doorway.

For the second time in her dream, or whatever it was, Holly was underwhelmed by what she saw. Once through the doorway, they were in a generic office building corridor. It was painted off-white and had a low neon-lit ceiling and grey industrial carpet. On either side, numbered doors were positioned every ten feet or so, giving the hallway a cold, clinical feel.

"Do you have a first name?" Holly asked, trying to lighten the mood.

"Yes," Ms Babbitt replied, without answering the question.

They walked in silence down the corridor until Ms Babbitt came to a sudden stop.

"We're here."

Ms Babbitt knocked then opened door number 3209 and held it open for Holly. Holly peered around the doorway and saw what, to all intents and purposes, looked exactly like a doctor's examination room. Weirder still was that the room inside was much bigger that she'd expected considering how close the doors were to each other in the hallway.

"Doctor Mitchell will be with you in a minute," Ms Babbitt said as she closed the door, leaving Holly alone in the room.

With nothing else to do, she began snooping. The first thing she noticed was that it had a full-sized examination table with steps at one end so that smaller patients could climb up. There were two patient chairs against the wall. One big and one half the size. On the walls were the usual array of charts showing the different parts of the human body together with all their names. Some showed the bones and musculature, while others showed the internal organs. There were two of each chart. Holly presumed that one was for elves and the other was for bigger folk. After studying a number of them, she saw that there was hardly any difference between the two types except for size.

Then she came to a chart showing a diagram of the chest. The one on the right looked like the ones she'd seen at doctors' offices on the rare occasions that she'd needed to visit one. The chart on the left, however, had one glaring difference. The elves' chart showed the heart as being exactly the same size as on the other diagram, yet the body itself was far smaller. She stood close to make sure that she was seeing it correctly.

"You're not mistaken," a voice said behind her. "They all have very big hearts, both figuratively and in reality."

Holly jumped and spun around. She hadn't heard anyone enter the room, yet standing in front of her was an older-looking man in a white coat with a stethoscope around his neck. He looked like Hollywood's idea of a small-town family doctor except that he was substantially shorter than Holly.

"I'm Doctor Mitchell," he said as he held out his hand.

"Are you an…" Holly started to ask before stopping herself. "Sorry. That was rude."

She shook his hand.

"Not at all. I'm somewhat of an anomaly here and am used to the occasional sideways glance. To answer your question, I'm an elge. That's a cross between an elf and a large person. My dad was a large person. He was one of the two hundred or so that work for NPMD for when they need someone to interface with the world at large. Get it?" he chuckled. "World at large?"

Holly managed to force a smile.

"Anyway," Mitchell continued, "Elves and large people are not supposed to mix. At least not in that way. Despite the policy, one day when my dad was helping repair a piece of equipment in the cafeteria, he looked up and saw Annie, that's my mom, for the first time. Darn it if they didn't fall for each other right there next to the broilers and heating trays. They tried to keep it quiet but having a large man sneaking around the complex became pretty dang obvious."

"Why weren't they allowed to mix?" Holly asked.

"It's not that it's not allowed, it's just strongly suggested that elves and large people refrain from serious relationships. The problem is that, because of the rift, elves live incredibly long lives. As large people usually remain living on the other side, their bodies are subject to all the rigours of ageing and then, of course, death. Not really a good plan for a couple wanting to age together."

"What do you mean that elves hardly age because of the rift?" Holly asked in a confused voice. "That's the second time I've heard that."

"Gosh darn it," Mitchell said, slapping his side. "You haven't had the briefing yet, have you?"

Holly could only shake her head.

"Forget that I said anything."

"What happened to your parents?" she asked. "Did they find a way to stay together?"

"I'm here, aren't I?" he laughed. "My dad made the ultimate sacrifice and gave up the outside world so he could stay here with my mom."

"Why couldn't they..." Holly started to ask.

"I've said too much already. It's time to give you a quick check-up before you go to your next appointment."

"You want to examine me?" Holly asked.

"Just a basic once-over," Mitchell assured her. "Nothing invasive, I promise you. I'm just gonna check your vitals."

"Why?" Holly asked.

"I really can't go into that," he responded.

"You're going have to or I won't let you examine me."

Mitchell gave her a long pondering look.

"It's procedure before you go any further into the facility," he finally admitted.

"Why?"

"We want to be sure that you're in good health and don't have a heart attack and drop dead," he stated bluntly.

"Why would I drop dead?" Holly kept on at him. "Is this rift thing going to be that dangerous to my health?"

"Heavens, no. It's safe as houses. We just don't want you dropping dead from shock at what you're about to see."

Holly carefully studied the man's face trying to find any indication that he was joking.

She saw from Doctor Mitchell's expression that he had been completely serious.

"You'd better get started, then," Holly said as she walked over to the examination table.

CHAPTER
FOURTEEN

The doctor had been true to his word. The examination was quick, professional and totally respectful. The moment he had finished, the office door opened, and the ever-cheerful Ms Babbitt could be seen waiting impatiently in the corridor.

"Hurry up," she said as she tapped one foot repeatedly. "We can't be late."

"I haven't heard the results yet," Holly stated.

"That's between the doctor and boss," Babbitt barked.

"I have every right to know the results of my own physical."

"Oh, for Heaven's sake," Babbitt sighed, clearly frustrated with Holly's demand.

"You're healthy as a Kork," Dr Mitchell revealed.

"What the heck is a Kork?" Holly asked.

"That's enough of this tomfoolery." Babbitt actually stamped her foot in a show of peevishness.

Holly took her time thanking the doctor and putting back on the heavy coat she'd been given in the sleigh.

"There's no need for that in here," Babbitt snapped.

"You never know," Holly replied. "I might just decide that I've had enough of your rudeness and go back outside."

"Silly girl. You really don't have a clue, do you?"

Holly stuck her tongue out at the elf as if she were five. Holly didn't care what Ms Babbitt thought of her. This was her dream, and she wasn't going to let some grumpy elf ruin it for her.

Babbitt let out another frustrated sigh, then led Holly further down the corridor to another identical door. She knocked, then opened it and gestured for Holly to go in.

The room was a completely different size from the examination room and couldn't have looked more different. The walls were lined with dark wooden bookshelves that went as high as the ceiling. On display were books that were focussed on every aspect of psychiatry and psychology. A small leather-topped desk and swivel chair sat at one end of the room. A full-sized overstuffed sofa sat at the other end.

"The doctor will be with you shortly," Babbitt advised as she shut the door behind her.

Holly grinned. The room looked like something out of a comedy sketch about Sigmund Freud. It was all too perfectly stereotypical. She read a few of the book titles and smiled. They were hysterically funny, at least to her.

To Be or Not to Be...The Unanswered Existential Question, The Id of Your Ying and Yang, Can Super Egos and Super Computers Co-exist?

She was about to pull that last one off the shelf when the door opened and the doctor walked in. Holly didn't know where to look. He was an older human and was wearing a red velvet smoking jacket, a pair of pince-nez spectacles and a pair of black satin slippers. He had a white goatee and matching untameable hair.

"Good morning, Ms Hillman." He spoke with a harsh German accent. "My name is Doctor Poofman. I am going to ask you a series of questions in order to gauge whether your mind is capable of accepting the realities of what awaits you later on today."

"And if I fail?" Holly asked, trying desperately to not laugh.

"There is no pass or fail in psychiatry," Poofman replied. "There is only being."

Holly snorted before she could stop herself.

"I'm glad you find all of this amusing," Poofman stated. "That shows that you have the ability to shield your psyche from the inexplicable. After what you have already seen today, most people would already be experiencing some degree of mental anxiety."

"That doesn't make any sense," Holly said. "All of this is just a dream. There's no way that any of this could harm me or anyone else."

"Aha!" Poofman exclaimed. "You have protected yourself behind a delusionary premise. Again…that is a healthy sign."

Poofman gestured for Holly to sit on the sofa as he slid his swivel chair next to it.

"Tell me about your childhood," Poofman began as he plopped down on his chair.

The session took almost an hour. Holly had no idea how she'd done. Poofman had shown no emotion as she answered his questions and his expression never seemed to change. As much as she'd tried, he was impossible to read. Then, without any preamble, he stood up, thanked her for her patience and walked out the door. Seconds later, Ms Babbitt appeared and asked Holly to follow her to the next and last appointment.

Holly couldn't even begin to imagine what they could check her for at that point.

"What's next?" Holly asked. "Please tell me it's not the dentist."

"Of course not," Babbitt replied as they marched down the corridor. "At least not until you've been cleared by our proctology department."

"That's not going to happen," Holly announced, stopping dead in her tracks.

Babbitt turned around at stared at her. A smile, or at least what Holly assumed was a smile, appeared on the elf's face.

"Was that a joke?" Holly asked, feigning shock.

Ms Babbitt nodded almost shyly.

"I felt that you'd had a hard enough day so far. You have no more examinations. You are now going to have your temporal dimensionality orientation."

"You make that sound very serious," Holly remarked.

"It is." Babbitt smiled as she and Holly continued on down the seemingly never-ending corridor.

They reached door number 4024. Babbitt knocked and the door was opened by Gunnar Hyertol.

"Gunnar," Holly exclaimed. "What are you doing here?"

"Sorry to disappoint you, Ms Hillman, but I'm not Gunnar. I'm Petar Hyertol. I'm Gunnar's brother."

"That doesn't make any sense," Holly stated bluntly.

"Come in and make yourself comfortable. I have a lot of things to tell you that will hopefully answer all of your questions."

Holly stepped into the office. It was much larger than the others she had just been in and had floor-to-ceiling windows that looked out over Manhattan and, beyond that, the East River. It dawned on that the view was startlingly familiar, till it hit her that she was standing in her own apartment.

"Don't be alarmed," Petar said as he gestured for her to sit in what to Holly appeared to be her own cream-coloured armchair.

Holly sat as she continued to look about the room. It was exactly like hers.

"Before we start, I'd like to offer you a welcome cup of hot cocoa," Petar offered as he held out a dainty china cup and saucer. In it was rich dark chocolate.

"I'm confused," Holly replied weakly.

"Drink the chocolate," he coaxed.

Holly shrugged and drank it down in one.

"Yum! That was intense."

Holly handed the cup back to Petar, then suddenly sat up straight in her chair.

"What's going on?" she asked. "I feel strange."

"That will only last a second," he assured her.

Holly closed her eyes and leaned forward.

"The dizziness will also be gone in a few moments."

Holly slowly lifted her head and opened her eyes. She looked around the room, then up at Petar.

"How did I get back to my co-op and what the heck are you doing here, Mr Hyertol?"

Petar simply smiled at her.

"Wait a minute," Holly said as she shook her head. "I have been dreaming the strangest things and you were in…no. It wasn't you. It was your brother."

"Firstly," Petar began as he sat across from her. "you were not dreaming. You were given some milk and cookies earlier on…"

"In the sleigh," Holly remembered.

"Yes. In the sleigh. You were given a high dose of a harmless substance that we synthesise from the Theobromine that's found in dark chocolate. It has the effect of making one incredibly relaxed. Most people find that they believe themselves to be dreaming."

"You drugged me?" Holly barked as she got to her feet. "I'll sue you and your…your…whatever the heck this is for every dollar you have."

"Sit down, Ms Hillman, and let me explain," Petar said soothingly.

"If you think I'm going to…"

"Holly…sit down, now," Petar commanded as if to a trained dog.

Holly instantly sat, yet didn't know why she'd followed his instruction.

"You will give me five minutes to explain everything before you refuse to listen," he stated. "Understood?"

Holly didn't even remotely understand, yet found herself nodding.

"When you were in the bar at your hotel, you met Blit and Donna. You then began to drink what you thought to be a liqueur called Black Death. You drank until you believed you were highly inebriated. You were not drunk at all."

"But I distinctly remember…" Holly tried to interrupt.

"The bartender had given you a carafe of iced water laced with a super concentrated form of camomile. It made you woozy and open to suggestion. That was how they managed to get you to agree to go for a drive."

"Are you saying that I've been drugged twice?" she scolded.

"Actually, if you include the antidote that was in the hot chocolate you just drank, it would be three times…no, wait…then there was the peppermint vapour in the SUV, so you'd have a little sleep."

"What is wrong with you people?" she barked at him. "Wait a minute. If all that's true, why are we in my apartment?"

"We're not," Petar replied. "We created this space to try and make you feel more comfortable. More at home."

"If this isn't really my home and we're not even in New York, then where the heck are we?"

"Please let me continue," Petar insisted. "Once you got into the vehicle in Nuuk, you were brought to the northernmost point of what is referred to as the North Pole. You were then passed through an annex, or air lock, if you like, between your home dimension and the one you are currently sitting in."

Holly gave him a "You must be kidding" look.

"The reason you are here is so that you can meet the man who may well be your father."

"The man who drugged and kidnaped me?" Holly said. "Sounds like a father-of-the-year candidate already."

"Just for the record, you were not forced to come here. You were made to feel calm and accepting. That's all. You could have said no."

Holly rolled her eyes.

"Perhaps it's best at this point for you to hear who your father actually is."

"Okay. Time for the big reveal, huh?" she said sarcastically. "Who the hell is he? He's not some crazy old reclusive nutjob, is he?"

"Not exactly," Petar replied in a calm tone.

"Then who is he?" Holly asked.

"Do you want his real name or the one that you would recognise?" he offered.

"I'll take option two," Holly replied.

"I'll need you to take three deep breaths and hold the last one in while I respond."

"Why," Holly asked.

"In order that you don't immediately hyperventilate and pass out."

Holly looked closely at Petar, trying to see some trace of humour, hoping that he'd been joking.

She saw no trace whatsoever.

Holly took three deep breaths and held in the third one. Petar smiled.

"You know him as Santa Claus," he stated bluntly.

Holly blew out the breath and laughed.

"What the heck are you people playing at? If I am here to meet my supposed father, why all these ridiculous antics?"

"Because his situation is not a normal one," Petar explained. "We are not playing games. We are trying to bring you back together with the world's most famous and yet secretive person."

"I get that," Holly responded. "Just stop messing me around with all this nonsense about Santa and the North Pole and tell me who he is."

There was a loud knock on the door.

"I think I can do better than that," Petar replied. "Go see who's there."

Holly gave him a questioning look, then walked to the door.

She opened it and felt the axis of her world tilt violently.

The man standing before her had to grab her, fearing that she was about to fall over. As Holly collapsed into his arms, she could smell peppermint and cinnamon as his white bushy beard rested on her head. Her cheek was pressed against his bright red suit, trimmed with white faux fur. Her first reaction was that someone was playing a trick on her but as she looked up into his astonishingly blue eyes she recognised him from when she was a very young child.

"Santa?" Holly managed to ask.

The man nodded.

"Pappa?"

He nodded again, only this time he had to wipe tears away from his eyes.

CHAPTER
FIFTEEN

Petar and Santa gently guided Holly back in the room and into her armchair.

"Before we go any further," Santa said in a deep baritone voice, "may I please look behind your right ear?"

Holly looked confused by the odd request but nodded anyway. Santa leaned over and carefully folded her ear forward. Petar approached and moved aside some of Holly's hair. Santa pointed at a spot just above where the ear joined her head. A tiny, dark brown birthmark, no bigger than a kidney bean, was plainly visible on her skin. It was shaped like a candy cane.

Seeing the mark had an immediate effect on Santa. He staggered back and had to sit down until he could catch his breath.

"Are you alright?" Holly asked.

"I'm fine, just full of too many emotions for one man," he replied.

"What were you looking for on my ear?"

"Your birthmark," he replied.

"Was it there?"

"It most certainly was." He nodded.

"So, I really am your daughter?"

"Without question."

"How is that even possible?" Holly said shaking her head. "You can't be real. This can't be real."

"It is real – all of it. Just not in the way you were led to believe," Santa explained.

"That's just it. I was raised to never believe in anything like Santa or elves or fairies. I was raised in a very strict Christian household that only believed in God and Jesus."

"There's nothing wrong with believing in Jesus. He was a good man."

"You knew him?" Holly asked.

"No, my dear. I'm nowhere near that old, but I know of his teachings," he continued. "I am always saddened when I hear of a child who's not permitted to think like a child. It's an important stage of development. It allows one to have an open mind at least at that stage of life. As you get older, reality sets in and takes over."

"But aren't you trying to convince me that you really are Santa? That would require one heck of an open mind, wouldn't it?"

Santa laughed. "Yes, it would, and the fact is that I do exist but, as I said, not in the way most people think of me. Petar, do you mind if I take over the orientation? I think I can manage it."

Petar smiled knowingly. "Of course. I'll leave you both alone."

Once Petar was gone, Santa moved his chair closer to Holly's and began to speak.

"First things first; I should introduce myself. My real name is Otto Beenhouer. I was a crew member on a trading ship out of Amsterdam. It was 1642 and when we left the port we thought that we would be sailing the usual route to India. We had made the same trip a few times for the Dutch East India company, and me and the rest of the crew were not that concerned about the journey. We had a fine ship and an experienced captain. What we didn't know was the that the owners had something different in mind. They had given the captain and the ship's officers instructions to find a new, faster route via the Orient. To achieve this, they had to find a way to navigate over the top of the world."

"I'm sorry," Holly stopped him. "1642? You're telling me that you're 380 years old?"

"A little more than that. I was twenty-nine when we left port." He smiled. "Let me finish the story before you ask any more questions. I think you'll find that everything will make more sense afterwards. Well, maybe not sense, but you'll have a better understanding of me and all of this."

"I'm listening," she replied. "Not sure I'm believing, but I am listening."

"We sailed up the west coast of what is now Greenland, at which point the captain finally had to tell us his plans. We reached what is now Baffin Bay with the intent of hugging the Canadian shore hoping to find deep enough open water to take us through the Arctic Circle. A storm developed in the bay. It grew into a monster. Nobody on board, neither the crew nor the officers, had ever seen anything like it in their lives. Even with our sails reefed all the way in, the wind ripped them from the masts before taking them as well.

"A rogue wave took our rudder and anything and anybody that wasn't secured on deck. We were adrift in a fifty-foot sea. We had no control and no idea of exactly where we were. The storm lasted three full days and nights and took with it sixty good men. Twelve of us survived but we were all suffering from exposure and hunger. The ship, or at least what was left of her, somehow found its own way up an uncharted and unfrozen tributary and grounded less than a hundred miles from where Travis met you when you landed.

Holly was about to speak when Santa gestured with his hand for her to hold off a little longer.

"By the time I stepped onto the ice, I was the only crew member left alive. I took as many warm garments as I could wear and even managed to put one set of boots inside another to try and keep my feet as warm as possible. What stores hadn't been destroyed or washed overboard I dragged behind me on a length of ripped sail. I had a compass but found that the darn thing didn't seem to work that far north. I knew nothing of magnetics and the like, just that it was of no use to me.

"I started walking. I stopped for rest breaks when I could find some shelter from the constant wind. Usually, it was just a raised piece of displaced ice from a shattered flow that afforded me the luxury of some still air. I don't know how long or how far I walked, but I remember that my food was almost gone as was my will to continue. I can still recall the day when I stopped walking. I had gone as far as my body could take me. My strength had gone, and exhaustion consumed my emaciated body. I kneeled and said a small prayer for my soul then laid myself down on the ice and closed my eyes.

"I had intended for that to be the end of me, but the cosmos had different plans. The place where I had collapsed was only a few metres from one of the openings to the dimensional rift…"

Holly opened her mouth to speak.

"Which I will shortly explain to you," he said, cutting off her interruption. "I actually believed that I had died and passed on. I felt hands lift me into the air and I knew I was soon to pass through the gates of Heaven. I woke up some time later and found myself to be in a makeshift bed, covered in colourful quilts. My hands and feet were bandaged, and I knew then, with surprise and even some regret, that I was still among the living.

"I was unable to stand, but each time I fell back asleep I would wake up to find that food and water had been left next to my bed. It wasn't until the fourth day that I finally met my first keeper of the Elfissional Rift. You have met some today. In modern times they are referred to simply as elves. That first elf stayed with me for many long hours explaining where I was and what it meant to be within the rift."

Santa could see that Holly was bursting with questions.

"Before I continue with the story, I have to explain the rift, otherwise nothing else will make any sense. You might want to take a break now, if you're in need."

"A toilet break would be nice," Holly replied.

"Step into the hall, turn right and after about sixty

metres or so you will see two brightly painted doors on the left and two on the right. The ones on the right are for ladies. The first door is for elf use, the second for larger folks. You'll see that the sign is twice as big on the second door."

Holly started to get to her feet.

"Please don't open any other doors in the hallway at this time, not until you understand fully where you are," Santa requested. "Remember, this is room 4024. Don't get lost."

Holly nodded her understanding and let herself out of the room and into the corridor. She found the ladies' room where Santa said it would be and let herself in. Holly was disappointed and a little surprised that the room looked boringly like any public bathroom and wasn't the slightest bit otherworldly as she'd hoped.

The room had six plain white pedestal sinks, six cubicles, and a paisley sofa against one wall. Holly thought that she was alone in the room but once she'd settled in her cubicle strange sounds started coming from the one next to hers. Initially it was just a guttural clicking sound, but after a few moments it got louder and turned into what sounded like a dog yipping. At one point the cubicle dividing wall suddenly started rattling.

"Are you alright in there?" Holly asked with concern.

"Yes. Sorry." The voice was deep and manly and almost had a sing-song quality to it.

Holly heard the person open their cubicle door and walk to the sinks. There was an inordinate amount of splashing and what sounded like gargling. Finally, the person activated one of the wall driers. After a few moments, Holly distinctly heard the sound of purring.

When Holly stepped back out into the hall, she was momentarily disorientated and turned the wrong way. She stated walking down the hallway looking for room 4024 but none of the numbers were even close, nor were they in any particular order.

Frustrated, she finally knocked on one of the doors, then opened it.

Holly was standing on the brink of space. There was nothing beyond the open door except blackness and the occasional distant star. It looked nothing like any starfield that she'd ever seen before. It somehow appeared far more vast and infinite.

"This room's occupied," a voice boomed back at her.

"Sorry," she gasped as she shut the door.

Holly managed to retrace her steps back to the bathroom and headed the right way back to her orientation room.

"Everything alright?" Santa asked as Holly walked into the room. "You look a little frazzled."

The last thing she wanted to do was to admit to having looked into one of the rooms after he specifically had told her not to.

"There was someone in the cubicle next to me and whoever it was was making the strangest noises. I'm pretty sure it was a man and at one point he suddenly started yipping like a small dog."

Santa laughed. "That wasn't a man, though the Wooblegangers do have very masculine voices to our ears. We offer an exchange student programme between the elves at our university and the Wooblegangers from a different rift. They at first can seem to be rather odd creatures but they're terribly bright and once you get to know them they have a very sharp wit and silly sense of humour."

Holly sighed deeply.

"I took the liberty of having some cookies and milk brought by," Santa said, gesturing to a laden tray on a side table. "You must be a little peckish."

"I keep getting offered milk and cookies. Is that all you eat in this place?"

"You'll have to forgive me; I am used to spending most days with elves. Something about their metabolism makes them crave sugar. All the time. You might find this hard to believe, but when I arrived here I was as thin as a rail. Look at me now."

Santa patted his stomach.

"You've had 380 years to perfect it," Holly commented.

"Aah, if only that had been the case. I got to be this size my first year here. Back then the only food available was what the elves ate. Now of course we have a full cafeteria that serves any type of cuisine you can imagine."

"Even Woobleganger food?" Holly asked.

"Absolutely," he replied. "I find it too salty and have never been comfortable eating things that are that shade of green, but, considering where they come from, it's not that bad."

Holly reached for a cookie and was about to take a bite when a thought hit her.

"Are these okay to eat or am I due for another anti-anxiety drug?"

"They are perfectly safe," he advised. "Look."

He reached over and grabbed a cookie and a frosted glass. He took a big bite, then washed it down with the milk.

"Have you ever thought of dieting?" Holly asked.

"I used to diet on and off. Now it's not possible. I'm a branded item. The red suit, the beard and the girth are all trademarked."

"I thought Santa Claus was public domain?" Holly said.

"That's what everyone thinks but through some clever accounting and just a little rift magic, everyone who sells anything connected with me and the brand pays a .01% royalty fee. Nobody even notices, yet it's enough to help finance our little operation."

Holly took a bite of her cookie and rolled her eyes with pleasure.

"It's the extra molasses that does it," Santa said with a smile.

Santa let Holly finish, then resumed the orientation.

CHAPTER
SIXTEEN

"Let's start with the rift. First you need to understand that there are alternate dimensions to your own. Some are parallel and bear similarities to your dimension, but others are astoundingly different. The elves come from one of those. They have no home world such as we do, and, even more strangely, they have no knowledge of their creation or evolution. They simply exist. They are assigned throughout their dimension as keepers of the various rifts that offer passage between their dimension and thousands of others. There are only a few entry points to this rift here on earth and maybe a few thousand within our universe, but within dimensional universes there are millions. Some rifts lead from relatively safe dimensions like ours. But some offer access to and from places and planes that cannot even be described.

"The elves...I should mention that I gave them that name as they didn't have a term for themselves. As our rift was called the Elfissional Rift, I basically named them after it. When I found myself inside their dimension, I learned that I stopped ageing, well, not stopped exactly, but certainly slowed way down. Time within their dimension does not exist as we know it. In earth's dimension we think of there being a past, a present and a future. Here we coexist with all three at the same time and can move between them. The other initially unnerving thing is that, though you and I appear to be carrying on at our normal earthly pace, time, if you want to call it that, moves at a completely different rate. You may be interested to know that, back at the place where you first encountered Travis, as far as anyone observing who is not within the rift, you still haven't stepped out of the sleigh."

"That's not possible. I remember Travis opening the door and leading me inside. I specifically remember stepping out of the sleigh." Holly insisted.

"We're getting into the field of quantum relativity here. I've never been smart enough to really understand it despite how many times the elves try to explain it but let me use your arrival as an example. The landing area outside is still within range of the rift effect. It is not the portal, but still is affected by some of the radiant energy from the rift dimension. Because of that, until you had passed through the actual portal, you were in fact interacting with both dimensions at once."

"Are you saying that, if I'd looked back at the sleigh, I would have seen myself still sitting there?" Holly asked.

"Yes," Santa explained. "In that spot, both dimensions were overlapping yet independent, in effect creating two Hollys. One entered the portal in my dimension, the other one remained in hers because of the relatively reduced speed of the passage of time."

"So, time moves slower outside the rift?" she asked.

"Not exactly. Outside the rift, time moves in a linear fashion, whereas in here time is simply whatever you relate it to."

"Are you sure you didn't put something in my milk? This all sounds impossible."

"I did not," he assured her, "and I promise you that it is all very possible."

"Before I even attempt to get my head around all this relativity stuff, I want to know how the red SUV left Nuuk with three people yet arrived here as a sleigh with only me inside and two reindeer pulling it?"

"Finally, a question I can answer with some degree of understanding." Santa smiled. "In the dimension where I live and you are currently visiting, there is a race of beings that are able to move freely through time and space creating their own secure vortices. They are also able to adjust their form into anything they want."

"Donna and Blit actually transformed themselves into reindeer?" Holly asked, amazed.

"Actually, it is the other way around. The reindeer shape is the natural form of the Korks. The humans you met were what they transformed into."

Holly closed her eyes as the various pieces of information she'd recently learned began to dovetail and collate into something vaguely akin to understanding.

"Is all this related to how you are able to deliver gifts around the entire world in one night?"

"Not quite but we're almost to that point," he replied

proudly. "Let me finish the explanation, and then I think you will find that all the pieces fall into place."

Holly grabbed another cookie and bit off half as she looked to Santa to carry on.

"Where was I…oh yes; so, the elves nursed me back to health then gave me a choice of where I wanted to live. I'd become very helpful within the rift doing odd jobs, heavy lifting and any chore that required height. That was actually the main reason why they made me an extraordinary offer. They would help me leave the rift and return to my old life or I could stay within the rift and have a completely new one."

"It just dawned on me," Holly interrupted. "How were you able to communicate with the elves? The world, even back then, had hundreds of languages. It seems unlikely that they would speak Dutch."

"Fair point," he conceded. "When they took me in, I was astounded to learn that the human race is the only civilisation that still communicates solely using mouths and ears. All the others, except some dreadfully primitive slug-like entities in a rift billions of light years from here, communicate mainly by telepathy."

"But I've been speaking to a number of them since arriving and they were talking with their mouths."

"Are you sure about that?" Santa said smugly.

"Haven't they?" Holly asked.

"They move their mouths when talking to individuals who are new to telepathy just to make them feel more comfortable."

"But what if…"

"Please let me finish the story," he said gently, stopping her mid-question. "When they made the offer, I asked if

I could live with them for a while until I'd got a good feel for what life in the rift would really be like. They advised that I would have to decide soon because the effects of living in a different state of dimensionality would have long-term consequences if I chose to return to my original dimension. The lack of time flowing within the rift is highly beneficial to our organs and arterial system. If someone whose body had acclimatised fully to the rift then returned to their original dimension, it would have a horrific impact on their health and longevity."

"Are you telling me that I can't leave?" Holly asked.

"No, of course not. It takes much longer than the time you've been here."

"So, you do have time here," Holly stated, proud of the fact that she'd found a flaw in his explanation.

"Not as you know it but relatively speaking...yes."

"That doesn't make sense," Holly said. "You've been here for...wait a minute. You said that you first arrived in the rift 380 years ago. If time doesn't progress in the same way as where I'm from, and in your dimension everything is a thousand times faster than out there" – Holly pointed out the window – "380 years here must be only a few months in my world."

Santa laughed. "I'm afraid that you are thinking like a logistician. Time within the rift isn't moving in any one direction. It simply is. It's only when you move from this dimension to yours that you see that linear time beyond the rift has hardly budged at all. I only told you that I arrived here in 1642. You extrapolated the time that had passed between then and your present day...outside of the rift."

Holly chewed the other half of her cookie while trying to get her head around what he'd just said.

"I'm sorry but I have to ask a couple of questions before you go on with your explanation or I know I won't be able to completely follow what you're saying."

"Go on, then," he agreed.

"Do you actually deliver presents to children around the world?"

"Yes," he replied.

"Do you deliver them in one night?" she asked.

"Yes, but only as is perceived in your dimensional timeline."

"Just keep the answers to yes and no," she insisted. "Is it because time out there is moving so slowly that you are able to accomplish that?"

"Yes."

"Okay...if you spend that much time out of your dimension, why don't you get sick?"

"First of all, I am not out of my dimension, as you put it. If I were, I would be subject to the same laws of time that you are."

Holly put her head in her hands and pretended to scream.

"I don't understand what you're saying. Please start making some sense," she pleaded.

"It's the sleigh," he explained. "Just like I told you how the rift bleeds out into your dimension, the sleigh has been built with the ability to create a dimensional field around it. Basically, I take my dimension with me."

"Okay...I guess I have to accept that answer. But even if you stay in your dimension, and manage to get to the home of every kid in the world..."

"Only those who believe in Santa," he interrupted. "Don't ask me about that part yet. You'll see how that works later on."

"But you still must have to go to millions of homes, right?"

"Yes."

"Then answer me this…how do you go down chimneys in homes that don't have fireplaces?"

"Aah. The age-old question," he replied, amused. "Because of how slowly time is relatively moving in your dimension, the atoms that make up everything in your world are also greatly slowed down. Without going into too much detail, I am able to walk through walls."

"How?" she asked.

"Because the dimensional rift field only ever has half the force of the actual one, my body is not fully solid in the alternate dimension. Think of me when I'm inside the dimension field as something ghost-like, but more realistic looking. I only use that technology on your Christmas Eve, as I will be away from the rift for a long time. If I ever need to visit your dimension for an hour, let's say, I am my normal non-ghostly self."

"But if you stay in my dimension for even an hour, isn't that like a month in here?" she asked.

"Again, time does not exist as such here. It's all about relativity."

Holly could only stare at him.

"You're being serious?"

"Don't look so perplexed. It's not magic, it's just science."

"More like science fiction," she quipped.

"I promise you that eventually all this will become much clearer," Santa replied. "Do you have any more essential questions, or can I finish the story?"

"Just one. How did the belief that you climb down chimneys come about?"

"That was started by parents who thought it to be the only rational conclusion," Santa replied.

"I just thought of another question. When Proseq ran my DNA, they said that there was no familial match to any location. If I'm your child, wouldn't there be a trace of Dutch heritage?"

"Had I not stayed in the rift, then yes, my DNA would show ancestry in Holland," he explained. "The thing is, once I remained within the rift, and my organs adapted to it, my blood and even DNA changed dramatically. What Gunnar never told you was that the reason your DNA showed no familiar match to anywhere on earth was because your DNA wasn't from earth. You were born in an interdimensional rift in both time and space."

"That's something one rarely hears," Holly joked.

"May I continue with the story?" Santa asked.

"Actually, for some reason, that did make me think of one more question," Holly said. "Why did you start giving gifts in the first place? And why on that specific day?"

"That, my dear, will be clear when you've heard the entire story. Ready?"

"I'm ready."

"I obviously chose to stay in the rift, otherwise we wouldn't be having this conversation," he chuckled. "After some time had passed, it became apparent to the others that I had grown despondent. One of the elves suggested that perhaps I would enjoy venturing out of the rift and visiting my home. I was stunned. I hadn't been aware that such a thing was even possible. I knew of the reindeer and their powers but never imagined that I could harness them to let me visit Amsterdam. When I had last put to sea, I left behind a raging drunk of a father who never appreciated me, and also a younger brother whom I dearly loved.

"The elves fashioned me a sleigh and two Korks were harnessed to the front. The elves also provided an early version of a dimensional field generator so that we could stay out of the rift for as long as I wanted. That was the day that I found out that that time beyond the rift moves at a vastly different rate. They explained to me that, though time hadn't seemed to move within the rift, and I believed that I had only been there a few weeks, outside many years had passed. I wasn't sure that I really believed the elves, but as we descended out of the clouds I could see that Amsterdam had drastically changed. After we landed I saw signs in shop windows and on buildings that warned of the plague. I walked to our house with the intent of leaving a few gifts that the elves had made as well as some chocolate that they produce only once a year. I found our house to have been painted black and had the word plague written on the outside. The house was in disrepair and without occupants.

I had been gone in their time for twenty-three years, yet thought only a few months had passed. I was heartbroken and was ready to return to the rift when I heard crying coming from a neighbouring house. I looked through the window and saw three children sleeping in front of a coal fire with only greyed and cold embers in the grate.

"I forced my way into my boarded-up family's home and filled a sack with coal that was stored in the kitchen. I returned to the home of the children and placed the coal next to their hearth. I then left the chocolate and one of the carved wooden gifts in front of each child. Because of the dimensional relativity, they never saw me. It would have been hours later in their time before they even realised that gifts had been left for them.

Santa stopped for a moment to brush away a single tear.

"As I walked back to the sleigh I noticed a calendar hanging in a shop window. It showed the month as being December and, judging by the days that had been crossed out, it was the 24th."

"Christmas Eve," Holly said as she choked back tears.

"Yes. Christmas Eve."

Later, after Holly returned from another trip to the ladies' room; this one just to splash some water on her face just to make sure that she really was awake, Santa suggested they go for a walk.

"Is it safe...for me?" Holly asked.

"I wouldn't take you anywhere that's not," he reassured her.

"That brings up a huge point," Holly said as a thought invaded her consciousness.

She stopped and turned to face him.

"You've told me who you were and who are now, but there's one thing you haven't explained to me."

"What's that?" he asked.

"Why did you abandon me?"

CHAPTER
SEVENTEEN

"My dear child. I never did any such thing," Santa insisted. "Not that any blame can be given, but everything that transpired was your doing."

"How could I possibly…"

"Come with me," he said gently, cutting her off. "We'll talk on the way."

Santa practically shooed her out of the room, shut the door, then pressed an almost invisible button on the door frame.

"What was that for?" Holly asked.

"We're done with the room. I'm just letting central control know that it's available."

"Why would anyone else want to use a copy of my living room?"

Santa opened the door again. Inside was a plain, small, square room with a wooden desk and chair. Holly's apartment was gone, as were the floor-to-ceiling windows.

"We make sure to put each room back the way we found it," he advised as he started down the corridor.

Holly glanced once more at the door, then followed him.

"It was Christmas Eve 1981. I left the depot as always in time to begin deliveries the moment that children went to sleep in Tonga. They are the first to wake up on Christmas morning in your timeline. By the time I finished with American Samoa, the last stop for the night, I returned to the rift only to find the entire compound to be in a complete uproar. My wife greeted me at the runway in tears. Our daughter was missing."

"Hold on," Holly jumped in. "Your wife? I have a mother?"

Santa stopped and faced her.

"You had a mother. Sadly, she died many years ago."

"I thought you said that you live almost forever in the rift," Holly shot back.

"I did, but to do so, you have to stay within it."

"Then why did she leave?"

"She, ah...went looking for you," Santa stated.

"Why would she look for me outside the rift? I was two and a half. I was hardly likely to wander off into another dimension."

They had stopped beside another nondescript door.

"I'll show you why," he replied with a sigh.

Santa opened the door so that Holly could enter. Inside looked like a cross between Norad and the SpaceX flight control centre.

Row after row of complex-looking, elf-controlled monitoring stations radiated back from a wall that was made up of one massive video/data screen. Holly guessed that it had to have been at least a hundred feet wide by forty feet tall. One half of the screen was taken up with an exact rendering of earth laid flat. Holly correctly assumed that it was used to track Santa's progress on Christmas Eve. The rest of the screen was used for live video and data feeds from what appeared to be massive distribution hubs and support warehouses.

Santa walked up to a console and entered a few commands on a flat display. The entire wall screen went dark, then seconds later showed a video of what appeared to be the inside of some sort of aircraft hangar. It took Holly a moment to realise that she was looking at Santa's sleigh being prepped for flight. A date was visible on the bottom right of the screen. It read: 24/12/1982. EC.

"What's EC?" Holly asked.

"Earth Calendar," one of the elves answered.

Next to the sleigh, huge sacks of gifts were waiting to be loaded onboard. Suddenly, from off camera, a tiny child toddled over to one of the bags and peered inside it. The screen definition was such that her excitement was clearly visible on her face. She climbed into the sack only moments before a couple of elves loaded it together with dozens of others into the sleigh.

"Where was this video taken?" Holly asked in barely more than a whisper.

"Right here in the main hangar. I was restocking for another run within North America."

"Then what happened?" Holly asked.

I delivered twenty-eight million gifts on that final shift.

"That's not possible," Holly insisted. "The sleigh's not big enough."

"Of course it's not. We do mid-air restocking throughout the night. I only come back to base because it gives me a chance to relax for a few minutes and visit the men's room."

"Then you must know which homes you delivered to before restocking after your stop here," Holly stated.

Santa smiled. "Once the security team found this video, I went back to as many of those homes as I could, but there was no sign of you. We realised that, had you crawled out of the restocking sacks, you could easily have dosed off in the sleigh, then got into any one of thousands of sacks that were rotated in and out of the sleigh during the rest of the night.

"But what happened to me?" Holly pleaded.

"Once we found you after your DNA test, we were able to backtrack though sealed records," Santa explained, his tone serious and sad. "You were found asleep under a Christmas tree in a walk-up apartment in a run-down area of Newark, New Jersey. The family that lived there had never seen you before and had no idea how you'd got there. It seems that at some point during the delivery operation you managed to find your way into my red velvet sack, which I use when I'm actually entering the homes. It looks so much nicer that the burlap ones."

"Please stick to the story," Holly said testily.

"I think what happened was that you entered the apartment with me, either hiding or asleep in my red sack. As I was placing the gifts around the base of their tree, you must have snuck out and hid somewhere. I left that building and continued on with my work without any idea that I'd left my daughter behind."

"Once everyone back here saw the video, why didn't they contact you while you were delivering?"

"This was 1982," he replied. "There were no mobile phones, and we couldn't install any radios on the sleigh as it interfered with the dimension field, so it was normal for me to be out of communication for the entire operation. As you can see, they could track me from here and set up restocking to wherever I was, but there was never any direct communication. Besides, they only thought to check the hangar security recordings shortly before I'd completed the entire circumnavigation."

"So, you just gave up?" Holly asked, accusingly.

"Hardly," he replied. "We spent years trying every way we knew how to track you down, but, because of where and how you were found, the authorities were concerned that you may have been in some sort of danger. To make sure that nobody could find you, the police and social service's reports never mentioned that you were found abandoned in a stranger's home. The paperwork just said that you were removed from a family that couldn't care for you. Even then, all details about you were sealed."

"I'm sorry," Holly said. "I shouldn't have snapped at you like that."

"It's understandable," he replied softly.

"Tell me what happened to my mother."

"When all options failed to pan out, she made the decision to hire investigators and leave the rift so that she could be on hand within your dimensional time, just in case they found something."

"But she didn't survive," Holly said.

"No," Santa confirmed. "Leaving the rift was too much

for her system. She died within a couple of years of living on the other side."

"Did you know that she was dying?"

"Not immediately," he admitted. "She blamed me for what happened to you. We spoke a few times, but she made it clear that she preferred to not see me again."

"I'm so sorry," Holly said as her eyes started to tear up. "All of it really was my fault."

"You were two and a half. Nothing was your fault."

Santa opened his arms and Holly stepped into his embrace.

"What was my mother like?" Holly asked.

"She was very like you," he answered. "Independent, smart, driven and beautiful."

"I wish I'd known her."

"So do I."

"If I left the rift back then, why hasn't it affected my health?" Holly asked.

"You were very young. Your system was still growing. The transition to a new dimension had little or no effect on you."

Holly took that in and stared up at the giant screen. One of the data boxes caught her attention. It said simply: N. LIST.

"There isn't really a naughty list is there?"

"Of course, there is," Santa replied. "I'm not going to go to all this trouble to reward a bad child. That would be a terrible precedent."

"How do you keep track?" she asked.

"It used to be very difficult and time consuming, but now, with most homes having Wi-Fi, the elves have managed to create an undetectable piece of code in every phone or tablet that actually measures the niceness or badness of the children."

"But young children don't have phones or tablets," Holly pointed out.

"Yes, but their parents do, and, luckily for us, they spend inordinate amounts of time taking pictures or videos of them."

"What about the children in the poorer parts of the world who have no Wi-Fi or phones?" she asked.

"I'll let you into a little secret about them," Santa explained. "Very soon after I went from giving that first gift in Amsterdam to where we are now, I decided that children who are not lucky enough to have nice safe homes, to say nothing of running water and a roof over their heads, automatically go on the nice list."

"Wow. That's astonishingly caring of you," she said. "You really do make a great Santa."

"I hope so. I'm the only one. Well, the only real one anyway."

Holly jokingly pulled on his beard.

"Ouch" he said, smiling.

"Just checking." Holly grinned then noticed that all the elves were watching her and Santa interact.

"There's something else that I've been dying to ask. Why do the elves keep their hats on all the time?"

Santa laughed. "A very good question."

He turned to face the elves within the control centre.

"My daughter just asked me why you keep your hats on."

Every elf in the room smiled knowingly, then removed their woollen hats.

"Oh my," Holly gasped.

The elves all had thick, long, golden hair that stood straight up from their heads. The hair almost doubled their height.

"The hats are just to keep their hair out of the way. If they leave it out in the open, they become top heavy and tip over," Santa explained.

As the elves replaced their hats, Holly looked questioningly over at her father.

"You're not serious?"

"Of course, I am," he replied.

"Then why don't they just cut it?" Holly asked.

"They can't. Unlike us, their hair has nerve endings right to the very end of each strand. Even cutting a single hair is excruciatingly painful for them."

Holly looked stunned.

"You don't have to look so horrified," Santa said. "There's a plus side to that. Brushing their hair gives them a wonderful tingling feeling and helps keep them relaxed."

"How odd," Holly muttered.

"Not for them," he pointed out. "We should keep moving if we're to keep to the schedule. Do you want to have a look at the manufacturing centre and distribution hub?"

"Of course I do. That's my business."

"Fancy that," he said with a wink.

CHAPTER
EIGHTEEN

Santa led Holly out a side door and into what looked like an inverted fishbowl. Above and around them, beyond the glass, was space. Not the outer space that Holly knew from looking upwards or from film and TV. What she was looking at was completely different. There were many more visible planets, some of which were closer than the moon is to earth. Their colours were extraordinary and looked like they were lit from within. Beyond the planets, there were no distant stars as one would expect to see from earth. Instead, there was a dull, dark-red glow that seemed to be interlaced with black tendrils that quivered and undulated.

"What am I looking at?" Holly asked in a meek voice.

"That's the dimensional rift that we're in," he replied. "That red and black background that you can see is the actual rip in the space–time continuum."

"I don't think I like being able to actually see something so…alien," she said. "It looks terrifying."

"Let's get you out of the bubble, then you won't have to look at it anymore."

"Doesn't it freak you out?" Holly asked.

"It did initially, but now it's no different than when you are looking up and seeing the moon. You're not scared of that, are you? It's just there."

"Yeah but this is different," Holly insisted. "That thing looks dangerous."

"It's no more dangerous than living on earth, whizzing through space at 16,000 miles an hour under the light of a star that will, in a few billion years, burn itself out."

"Thanks a lot," Holly replied. "That makes me feel much better."

Santa led her to an area where a dozen or so tubes seemed to branch out from one end of the bubble. It looked like a hamster habitat she'd seen advertised on TV when she was a child.

They walked into the third one from the right and stood against an odd-looking curved wall. It seemed to be covered in aluminium foil. Within seconds, Holly felt a breeze rushing through the tunnel. She looked up in time to see what looked like a giant, grey, horizontal teardrop pull up next to them floating about six inches above the ground.

"Don't worry," Santa said. "These things are completely safe."

"That's good to know, but what is it?"

"It's what we use as transportation within the rift. It's a telepathic conveyance."

"Of course it is." Holly sounded dubious. "How do you get in the thing? It doesn't even have a door."

"Watch me," he said as he approached it and simply stepped up and walked through the side of it. Holly assumed that it was the same technology as she had seen when she first stepped into the rift.

She took a deep breath, then replicated exactly what her father had just done. One moment she was still on the foil-wrapped platform, the next she was inside a comfortable padded compartment. The sparse interior glowed a shade of red. Santa was grinning at her as he held on to a polished chrome pole that ran from the floor up to the ceiling.

"Stand next to me and hold this pole," he instructed.

"There's no windows," Holly observed nervously.

"There is no need," he replied. "Just put your hand below mine and concentrate on building 42."

Holly gave him a doubting glance, then reluctantly stood next to him and held the pole as instructed. She was surprised to find that it was very warm and, when she first touched it, she felt the tiniest vibration run through her hand. She forced herself to think of what Santa had said, at which point, the lighting changed to a light shade of green, then an instant later went back to red.

"We're here," Santa announced as he stepped right through the outer skin of the teardrop.

It took Holly a moment to digest the fact that they had moved at all. She let go of the pole and stepped out into one of the most startling places she'd ever seen. Where they had exited the teardrop was some sort of arrival and departure terminal. Elves were dashing every which way in what, to Holly, looked like complete chaos. After watching them for a moment longer, she saw that there was some sort of system. They never slowed for a second, yet they also never collided with each other.

Beyond the terminal was a massive factory floor. Holly had visited some of the biggest manufacturing plants in the world, but all of them put together could have fitted inside the one she was looking at. It was so vast that she couldn't actually see where it ended. It just went on and on.

She followed Santa to an observation platform that was cantilevered out above the workers. Holly looked on in utter bewilderment. From her new vantage point, she could see just how unique the place really was. Unlike what she was used to, where each employee's workspace was only inches from the next person's, here it was radically different. Each worker seemed to have over fifteen feet of workspace before the start of the next worker's area. The ones that she could see most clearly seemed to be assembling wooden toys. Beyond their work bench was a conveyor belt that wound its way throughout the entire factory. Once a part was complete, the elf placed it on the cushioned belt, and it went off to some other station for the next stage of the assembly.

That part of the operation wasn't that unusual. The part that literally took Holly's breath away was that the area behind each elf consisted of a small yet perfectly proportioned house with a garden. Family members were doing chores or just keeping the worker company. As she watched, employees would signal a co-worker that they were going to stop what they were working on, then wander into the house or garden and grab a drink or snack. Some even sat down for a chat as other elves picked up the slack.

In addition to the extra workspace and proximity of their homes and family, parks and recreation areas were dotted randomly throughout the factory.

To Holly's way of thinking, the entire process was against every rule of manufacturing. Productivity was always weighed against space used. In this factory, there was way more space dedicated to living and recreation than there was to where the work was carried out.

"Pretty impressive, isn't it?" Santa said, proudly.

"I don't know what to make of it," she replied. "Is this where you make all the toys?"

Santa roared with laughter.

"Hardly. This is one of ninety-two factories in the rift. They each make or assemble a particular type of product. This one obviously specialises in wooden toys."

"Ninety-two factories of this size?" Holly gasped.

"No, of course not," he answered. "Their size is relative to the manufacturing space needed. This is one of the smaller ones."

Holly was speechless.

"Some of the electronics facilities are over four times the size," he added.

"How many elves do you employ?" she asked.

"I don't employ any of them. I just give them a place to do what they love doing."

"Are you seriously telling me that you don't pay them anything? That's despicable."

"You don't understand." Santa tried to explain. "If they don't work, they die."

"You monster!" she gasped, recoiling from his words. "You kill them if they don't work. What are you?"

Elves stopped and stared at Holly shouting at Santa. It was something none of them had ever seen happen before.

"Don't be ridiculous," he replied, gesturing for her to lower her voice. "Elves have to work every single day, or they become despondent, depressed and usually pass away from something akin to a broken heart. Even before I arrived here, all they did was work. I tried to get them to stop occasionally and almost caused a riot. Think of them like sharks. If sharks stop swimming, they die. If the elves stop working, the same thing happens. The one concession I got from them was that, if they insisted on working every single day, I wanted to provide them with homes right here in the workplace so they could always be close to their families."

Holly looked up at him with a dubious expression.

"Don't take my word for it," he insisted. "Look at them. Do they seem the least bit unhappy?"

Holly looked down at the closest workers and saw that, far from being unhappy with their lot, they seemed to be enjoying themselves.

"Are you ready to see the distribution hub?" Santa asked.

Holly nodded. "Look, I'm sorry for accusing you of mistreatment...I don't know where that came from."

"No need to apologise. I'm actually rather pleased to see you come to the defence of the workers. From what I recently read, you don't have a history of doing that."

"That's not fair," Holly responded. "When have I ever mistreated employees?"

"I didn't say that you mistreated anyone," Santa clarified. "However, from what I know of your upcoming purchase of the Ling Chow Group, that could be seen as condoning mistreatment."

"You keep well informed," she replied bluntly.

Santa tried to look into her eyes, but she turned her head away.

"Can we go now?" she asked.

CHAPTER
NINETEEN

After another instantaneous journey in one of the teardrop vehicles they arrived at another gargantuan building. This one was multi-tiered and was the size of a small city. There were no spacious workstations with homes and gardens. For as far as Holly could see, there were tens of thousands of workers toiling at breakneck speed to get packages sorted, gift-wrapped and then sent to the correct dispatch bay. Instead of there being one meandering conveyor belt, as there was in the toy factory, the distribution centre had what appeared to be hundreds of them.

Holly looked on in astonishment at the mass of frenetic energy that was spread out before her.

"What happened to keeping the workers happy?" she asked sarcastically. "I don't see any houses or recreation areas."

"That's because they're not needed here," Santa explained. "Only the older elves who have no family work in the distribution centre. Despite any attempts to change the way they live, older elves only want to work. They rarely sleep and only stop for brief food and toilet breaks."

"That sounds to me like you are taking advantage of their goodwill."

"Not in the least. Elves hate to get older and find that the more they work when they reach their twilight years, the longer they actually live. Just like with the younger elves, all I did was give them a place where they can do what they want to do."

"I thought you said elves live forever."

"Not forever, but certainly a long time if they are kept working. The average age of the elves in this facility would be about 600 years old in your dimension."

"Couldn't you have made it any more comfortable for them? It just seems cruel."

"When we built this centre, I had designed it with exactly the same specs as the manufacturing centres. All elves get to choose whatever work they want to do. Something about the manic repetitiveness of distribution attracted the elder ones. Within weeks of it opening, we were plagued with complaints about all the wasted space and oversized, cumbersome work areas. The elves even signed a petition to have all the amenities removed so they could focus on the job at hand."

Before Holly could ask him another question, an older elf in a dark three-piece suit approached them. The effect of his business attire was diluted slightly by the pair of green suede slippers and matching woollen hat.

"Herringbone, how are you?" Santa asked with a warm smile.

Herringbone stared at Santa, who moments later burst out laughing.

"Do you mind not doing the telepathy in front of me? I find it most disconcerting," Holly requested.

"Sorry," Herringbone replied out loud. "I just told him that you can't be his daughter as you are too slim and beautiful."

"Thank you," Holly said, feeling embarrassed by the compliment and by her testiness over the telepathy.

"We've run the delivery data again," Herringbone continued to speak, "but I'm afraid the numbers are still not good. Unless we come up with a solution by Christmas Eve, we won't be able to get enough gifts delivered on that night."

"I'll come and see you later," Santa said. "Thank you, Herringbone."

Herringbone gave Holly a brief nod, then walked off.

"What was that about?" Holly asked.

"It's the result of overpopulation. When I started doing this in earnest, the world had less than half a billion people. Now it has eight. Last Christmas we just managed to fulfil all the gift wishes for the nice children who still believe in Santa Claus. This year, however, it's going to be difficult to get enough gifts delivered with the logistics and distribution facilities that we have now."

"Would you allow me to have a look at your data?" Holly asked. "Logistics and distribution is what I do. If you can give me all the specs for the facilities plus the quantities and turnaround times, I might be able to find you some wiggle room."

Santa sighed with relief. "I was hoping you'd offer.

You'll have that data on your laptop by the time you get back to your hotel."

"I can't wait to see it."

"Before you go, I thought you would like to see my home." her father asked.

"Am I leaving?" she asked.

"You'd better make a start soon. Even with all our technology, the weather outside can be…"

"Frightful?" Holly finished for him.

Santa laughed at her having thrown in the opening lyric from the Christmas classic "Let It Snow".

"But the fire is so delightful," he recited, adding the next line.

Santa took Holly on another instantaneous teardrop journey. They walked through a smaller bubble dome then arrived at a hallway, similar to the one she'd been in for her examinations and orientation. It was the same bland off-white colour and seemed to go on for miles. Numbered doors spread ten feet apart continued down the hall for as far as Holly could see.

They stopped at number 8212.

"Be it ever so humble," Santa said as he opened it for her.

Holly knew to not be surprised when she saw more than a small room beyond the door, but her father's home was not at all what she expected.

"I've seen this place before," Holly said as she stepped inside.

She looked around the living room and saw a fireplace off to the right with an antique brass diving helmet positioned on the hearth. To the left of the room was a black grand piano nestled next to a set of stairs that headed

153

to the upper floor. Beyond the piano and the rest of the room was a wooden terrace overlooking Malibu and the Pacific Ocean.

"Oh my God! Holly exclaimed, then laughed. "It's the beach house from *Two and a Half Men*, isn't it?"

"Well spotted," Santa replied. "Obviously, it's not the actual set from the TV series but I liked the look of the place, so I changed my old look to this."

"But how…this is like when I arrived and ended up in my New York apartment, isn't it?" Holly asked.

"Exactly."

"Do I even want to ask how you can do this? I mean, I want to know, but I somehow get the feeling that I won't understand the explanation."

"It's easier than you think, but obviously the technology is vastly more advanced than anything you have in your dimension," he replied. "I presume you are aware of 3D printing in your world?"

"Of course. We have one at the head office."

"This is basically 5D but at a scale that you wouldn't imagine possible. Unlike your technology, we don't need a solid object so that we can make a copy. We can do so entirely from an image or even a telepathic thought."

"Let's say that I kind of understand that," Holly said. "But how come these small rooms can be whatever size you want?"

"That's easy," he replied. "We just use spatial relativity. The rooms are designed to expand to fit whatever needs to be inside them."

"And I'm back to feeling like the dumbest kid in class again." Holly sighed.

Santa took her for a tour of the whole house including the beach. She asked him what made him choose the look from a 1990s sitcom as his home.

"I spend my life either in a dimension that has no views other than space or in the darkness as I deliver presents. I decided that I loved this house and the views of the ocean beyond. I'm sure I could have found something else, but at the time it caught my fancy."

"I'm still shocked that Santa would watch such a bawdy TV show," Holly commented.

"Don't forget, my brand may depict me as a noble and gentle soul, but I started out as a sailor on a Dutch merchant ship in the sixteen-hundreds. I was hardly a saint."

"Wait a minute." Holly held up a hand. "How are you able to watch TV at all in the rift?"

"Initially, when TV first started, we weren't able to get a signal out here, but, thanks to your planet's innumerable satellites, the elves found a way to pirate the signals and encode them into something that would play here. Strangely, the higher the definition of the signal, the easier it is for us to manipulate it and enjoy it in the rift. The only slightly annoying thing is that the signal we receive is fifteen light years behind what you are watching so we're not exactly current."

"Are you happy way out here in your dimension?" Holly asked.

"I could ask you the same thing, kiddo," he said with a smile. "I think the best answer is that one does what one can with what one has."

"What are you going to show me next?" Holly asked.

"Actually, you should probably head home now. We have a lot to talk about but there's plenty of time now that I've found you."

"I am a bit frazzled," she answered. "By the way. I am happy that you found me."

"Me too," he replied.

Holly saw her father's eyes mist over.

"Darn allergies," he joked.

Santa saw Holly to the dimensional annex, where they said their goodbyes. She gave him a huge hug, then followed Travis out onto the snow towards the waiting sleigh.

Once on board, she noticed a glass of milk and cookies.

"We didn't know if you wanted to sleep through the trip," Donner stated from within her harness. "The cookies are just there in case you get hungry."

"Thanks for the warning," Holly replied.

"Is there anything else you need?" Travis asked.

"I think I have more than I ever deserved," she answered. "You were right earlier. You did change my life."

Travis smiled and backed away as the sleigh began to move and gather speed. As it lifted into the air, Holly looked back and saw nothing but snow and ice. There was no trace whatsoever of what lay beyond the invisible portal.

"Does this sleigh have the dimensional field around it?" Holly shouted to the reindeer.

"No," Blitzen replied. "Just the transfiguration device so that it can change into vehicles that won't shock your people."

Holly was slightly taken aback by the term *your people*. She was, after all, Santa's daughter. That should make her as much one of them as anyone else.

The return trip took just under an hour, but, according to her watch, the trip and the entire day spent in the rift had only taken a few minutes.

Donner advised Holly that they were starting their descent and that, if she was ready, they would activate the transfiguration.

"Of course," she replied. "I'm looking forward to seeing it."

"Don't blink," Blitzen joked.

Hearing that only made Holly want to blink more.

Holly blinked. One second she was in the open sleigh snuggled under a pile of faux fur, the next she was back inside the luxuriously appointed red Range Rover with Donner and Blitzen in their human form in the front seats.

The normally earth-bound SUV glided down onto a deserted-looking service road, far from the prying eyes of any people. Blitzen drove onto a more trafficked route then, after rounding a low mountain pass, Holly saw the lights of Nuuk in the distance.

There was hardly anyone out on the streets and snow was still falling, just as it had been when she'd left. They pulled up outside her hotel.

"Thank you both for everything," Holly said. "I hope to see you soon."

"You will," Donner stated as she reached out of the SUV and held something out for Holly.

"That's my phone," Holly exclaimed in surprise. "I never even missed it."

"We discreetly borrowed it from you when you were sleeping on the journey north," Blitzen admitted. "We have to be careful about people taking photos, as I'm sure you can understand."

"We've added something to your home screen," Donner said. "It looks like the Uber app, but you'll notice that under the name there is a tiny sprig of holly."

"That was my idea," Blitzen threw in.

Donner rolled her eyes. "It works the same way as Uber but there's only one destination."

"Let me guess." Holly grinned. "The North Pole?"

Donner and Blitzen both nodded.

"Whenever you want to go back, just open the app, and it will show you where the nearest sleigh is located and how long before it will reach you."

Holly took the phone and thanked them both again.

Once back in the hotel, Holly made straight for the bar. She had some questions for Minik. As she approached the Skyline bar, the only bartender she could see was much older and more serious-looking that the one she wanted to speak with.

"Good evening, madam. What can I get you?" he asked.

"Is Minik here?"

The man looked confused.

"I don't believe that I know anyone called Minik that works in this hotel. Holly was about to argue the point when it dawned on her that, considering everything else that had happened that day, a non-existent bartender hardly rated a comment.

"I'll just have a Chardonnay, please," she said as she sat on the same bar stool she'd been on earlier. For a brief moment she considered a Black Death, but even the thought of the caraway seed-infused vodka almost made her retch.

When Holly returned to her room, she made straight for her laptop. She opened it and saw an email from a magazine called *Reindeer Monthly*. She opened it and saw an attached file. There was no text or explanation, just one file named, simply, NPMD. She opened it and saw it was password protected. The first half of the password was already filled in. It read. TWOIF. She closed her eyes and tried desperately to think of what code he could have used.

Then it came to her. TWOIF stood for *the weather outside is frightful*. Holly then entered the rest of the password, *but the fire is so delightful*, reducing it to BTFISD.

The folder opened.

CHAPTER
TWENTY

By the time Holly landed in Teterboro the following day and climbed into her waiting SUV, she knew all there was to know about her father's operation. She assumed it would be vast but had no idea just how big it really was. Then again, an operation that had to deliver half a billion gifts on one night by one person was bound to be complex. What surprised her was that she had already found numerous inefficiencies that could easily be slowing down or at least complicating over a quarter of all deliverables. She needed to find some serious quiet time so she could outline her own version together with the improvements that she thought would help.

Her father had already explained that the biggest issue was the continually increasing volume that still needed delivery on the same night. That one was new to Holly. She was used to restructuring logistical functionality in struggling companies, but all of those involved a yearly operational plan, not a one-night special.

In addition to the delivery efficiency problems, there was the glaring overspending keeping the non-rift hubs operational all year long, while only using them in earnest one to two months of the year. The non-rift employees were not elves and required salaries. Santa kept every single one of his workers employed for twelve months yet, for eleven of those, they either sat idle or practiced operational drills. One of the most unique issues was that none of the hub employees knew anything about their employer. They certainly had no clue that they were working for Santa Claus. They thought that they simply worked for an Amazon-type reseller who only delivered on Christmas Eve as some sort of a promotional sales stunt.

Thankfully, they didn't care who the big boss was. They were paid well, had health care, retirement plans and free housing for themselves and their family members. Holly was impressed at just how well all of Santa's workers were cared for, but, from a profit and loss standpoint, the whole business model was a nightmare.

Holly was still looking at yet another spreadsheet on her laptop as Paolo pulled up in front of MWL's building. Holly was surprised to see that there was no sign of any protesters. Instead of feeling any sense of relief, Holly was more concerned as to why they weren't there.

As Holly got out of the car, she stopped by the driver's window. Paolo lowered it and looked up at his boss with a concerned look.

"I just wanted to tell you how much I appreciate the good work you've done for me all these years," Holly said. "I'll see you later."

Paolo had no idea what to say to her. Holly Hillman had, in the eight years he'd been driving her, only spoken to her twice. Both times were after a trip to Greenland.

By the time she reached her office with her holly plant in hand, Will was already standing waiting by Charlene's desk.

"Where are all the protesters?" Holly asked without any hello or preamble.

"You told me to do something about them, so I did," he replied, following her into her office.

"What did you do?" she asked.

"I had our security people photograph all of them. When they asked why, they were told that they were going to all be subpoenaed as witnesses to the class action lawsuit being brought by the worker's union that covered all of Ling Chow's employees."

Holly looked at him in amazement. "Did you come up with that idea?" she asked.

"Yup."

"But you were on their side," Holly stated.

"I'm just trying to do my job as best as I can," Will said.

"Even if it's against your principles?"

"Even then, yes."

"I assume that there is no lawsuit?" Holly asked.

"No, of course not," Will replied.

"Are any of Ling Chow's employees even members of a union?"

"Of course not," Will responded. "They all know that if they got caught even speaking to any union representative they would be fired instantly."

"I'm not sure how I feel about you selling yourself out like that," Holly admitted.

"You made it clear before you went back to Greenland that I didn't really have much of a choice," Will replied. "Speaking of which, how did it go over there? Do we have all twelve DNA results cleared?"

"Yes. It turned out that there wasn't a problem in the first place. One of the executives had given Proseq the wrong birthdate so the data wasn't matching up," Holly fibbed.

"And you had to go all that way yourself to sort it out?" Will asked. "That seems like overkill."

"You know the deadline we're on," she said, sounding suddenly distracted. "I felt it was best that I be the one to put out the fire. And, as usual, I did."

"As things stand, other than all the due diligence verifications, we are almost done with our share of the action points. We should be in a position to waive the contractual contingencies before the October 12th, deadline."

Holly didn't comment or reply. She was deep in thought.

"You alright?" Will asked.

"Sorry...yeah," she answered. "I just realised that I have one more trip to make before I can sign off on everything."

Will looked concerned. "I'm not sure what that could be. All the contingencies at this point are to do with data verification. I don't understand where you think you need to go."

"I want to visit Ling Chow's hub facility in Weng Chi again. Only, this time, I want to go there without giving them any advance notice."

Will looked at Holly as if he didn't know who she was. "I don't know if that's even possible."

"Of course, it is. I'm the CEO of the company that's about to buy LCG and their facilities," Holly stated. "I have every right to stop by one of their facilities and make certain that everything is, as has been stated by their management."

"But what are you looking for?" Will still could not get his head around Holly's decision to fly halfway around the world to do a surprise visit at a facility in China.

"I want to see exactly how the staff are really treated," Holly announced.

Will was stunned.

"Since when has the treatment of foreign employees been something that you're concerned about? Is this something new?"

Holly looked surprised by his question. She chewed her lower lip as she tried to answer his question.

"Yes. I guess it is," she finally replied.

"Will you be taking a full review team like last time?" he asked. "If so, you need to let them all know. This will have to be done and dusted within the next few weeks."

"I'm not taking a review team," she stated bluntly.

"Well, you can't go alone. You know how the Chinese respond to single women travelling by themselves."

"I won't be going alone," she replied.

"That's a relief. Who's going with you?"

Holly smiled. "Pack warm clothes," she said.

The flight took just over 15 hours. The Gulfstream descended through a thick layer of smog before touching down at the Weng Chi private airfield. The sky was slate grey as Will and Holly walked onto the cracked tarmac. A black Dongfeng SUV was waiting for them. Inside was a driver flown in from Marshall Whiteman Logistics' South Korean facility, as well as Lee Park, one of their operations managers, who spoke most Chinese dialects fluently and would act as translator if required.

The pilot had only notified the airfield of their intent to land fifteen minutes prior to arrival. Holly had wanted the LCG facility to have as little advance notice as possible. The airport manager tried to keep the group from leaving the field, insisting that an immigration official couldn't get there for at least three hours.

As the airfield was on private property and they weren't planning to go anywhere except the distribution hub, they ignored the officious little man and drove off towards the looming grey walls of the Weng Chi hub.

The facility had extensive security but all of it was focussed on the perimeter. Nobody had ever envisioned an uninvited visitor landing on the private strip within the compound. They encountered a number of security vehicles during the two-minute drive but none of the guards knew what to do about the visiting Americans and simply watched them drive by.

They pulled up to the main entrance and were met by the executive management officer, Zhang Wei. She had never met him before, but he seemed to know who Holly was and didn't even attempt to talk her out of touring the massive operation. Then again, he had probably known about her arrival the moment the jet requested clearance to land. He had almost certainly called the LCG head office to get approval before the Gulfstream even touched down.

Zhang spoke slow and deliberate English with a heavy Cantonese accent. He showed the group the main distribution centre, which was, by non-rift standards, immense. Holly had seen it before, yet was still amazed that, despite the operation being in full swing, the massive space was eerily quiet. The workers seemed not to speak at all. They simply kept their heads down and focussed on their specific task. Even though there was an unscheduled VIP tour meandering through the facility, not one employee looked up at them.

After seeing all of the main distribution site, the group was taken to the staff cafeteria, where a dozen or so workers were eating and chatting happily with each other. One wall was taken up by hot and cold food trays. At the other end were urns filled with teas and even hot coffee. The tour then moved to one of the dormitory buildings where the workers lived while employed by LCG.

It looked the same as when Holly had been escorted there by Ling Chow himself. Each worker had their own enclosed room with a bed, desk and sink. It was small but clean and functional. The staff members whose space it was had put up family photos and a couple of cheery posters showing sun-dappled trees and streams.

Zhang began his "thank you for coming" speech, hoping to finish the impromptu tour, when Holly interrupted him.

"Thank you Mr Wei, but I've seen all of this before. This time I want to see the real cafeteria and the main dormitory block."

Zhang tried to tell her that she had just seen them.

"Mr Wei," Holly began in a warm and friendly voice, "please don't lie to me. After all, in a few months you will, in effect, work for me. As a rule, I get on very well with my employees...but only those that tell me the truth. Those that don't...well, let's just say that they don't stay an employee of Marshall Whiteman for very long."

Zhang suddenly looked nervous and confused. He had given the exact same tour hundreds of times but had never shown a visitor the "other" buildings.

"If you will excuse me for a moment," Zhang said. "I need to make a quick phone call."

"Actually, I don't excuse you, Mr Wei. You have sixty seconds to make a very important career decision. Either show me the areas I want to see or I will call Mr Chow and inform him that we are reconsidering the merger due to the unprofessional treatment we received from you."

Zhang was already pale, yet after Holly's words, he managed to go at least three shades lighter. After a few seconds of gut-wrenching deliberation, he forced a smile.

"Of course, you may see what you wish." He held out his hands in a show of mock innocence. "There is nothing to hide from you."

Zhang led them out of the main building and towards a colourfully painted wall a short distance from the distribution centre. He walked under a carved wooden archway that depicted small birds in flight. They reached a chain link fence that was covered in green nylon material that made it impossible to see what was beyond.

Zhang slid open a ten-foot-long gate. Beyond the decorative wall, the beautiful archway and the shielded fencing were six large, drab, eight-storey buildings. They were made of unpainted concrete and looked as if they had been in place for a while. Orange rust streaks ran down the walls from the many broken pipes and cracked gutters. All the windows were barred, yet safety netting was suspended outward below each of them on the higher floors.

Zhang advised them that it was to protect the workers from falling snow and ice in the winter months. Will and Holly both nodded their understanding even though they both knew that the netting was there to try to stop their workers from throwing themselves out of the windows in an attempt to end their lives.

Inside, the dormitory bore no relation to the "staged" one they'd seen in the main building. Here there were no private spaces. Cheap and rusting double bunks were bolted to the walls and floor wherever there was room to fit them, including in the hallways. There was no sign of any personal items whatsoever. All each worker had was one thin, stained mattress to call their own. They passed countless men from different shifts who were asleep, fully clothed beneath flickering neon lights.

The group walked through the sleeping areas in silence. It wasn't until they reached the communal toilet and shower area that Will couldn't contain himself any longer. Along one wall covered in cracked, yellowed tiles were about twenty, one-inch diameter rusted pipes that poked out of the stained tiled wall at waist height. Greyish water dribbled out of each one. Will assumed (correctly) that, for the water to be that colour, it must be recirculated to save money. The staff were basically being forced to wash in their own second-hand bathing water. If that wasn't bad enough, the other side of the room was the toilet area.

Fourteen holes had been rough-cut through ancient vinyl flooring. There were no toilets, just the gaping holes. The area around each of them was filthy and obviously rarely cleaned. There was nowhere for the user to stand where they wouldn't be splashed with their own waste.

To make matters worse, there was no sign of toilet paper anywhere.

"This is completely barbaric," Will said through clenched teeth.

"Please show us the cafeteria," Holly said without acknowledging his comment.

Zhang led them out of the building to a wood-sided, single-storey building tucked behind the dormitories. Inside, the building was bleak. Instead of a selection of food and beverages, one large commercial-sized stewing pot sat on a single gas burner. Next to it were cheap cracked plastic bowls. There was no sign of chopsticks or any other form of cutlery. On a wall next to the pot was a single tap poking out of the wall. A tin cup was chained next to it. That was the drink selection.

Despite the horrific Dickensian look and feel of the place, dozens of young men were dotted around the untreated wooden tables. Every one of them was asleep with their heads resting on their arms. They looked worn out, mistreated and malnourished.

Before Will could voice his opinion of the conditions, Holly spoke.

"Thank you, Mr Wei. This has been very enlightening.

169

To save you any embarrassment with your employer, I won't say that you showed us this area."

Zhang looked relieved. For one awful moment, Holly was afraid that he was about to cry.

CHAPTER
TWENTY-ONE

Fifteen minutes later they were in the air, heading home. Will was still furious and desperately wanted to discuss the situation with Holly. They'd only been onboard the jet for thirty seconds when he let loose.

"I'm sorry. I know this could finish me at Marshall Whiteman, but you can't seriously be thinking of getting into bed with a company that treats people that way."

Holly went to the small kitchenette at the front of the plane and retrieved a sealed white box from an under-counter refrigerator.

"I'm going to eat. Do want yours yet?" she asked.

"How can you eat after what you just saw?" he shouted. "I knew you were cold, but this is too much."

"Please calm down and eat something," Holly said, ignoring his outrage. "We've got one chicken lunch box and one beef. Which do you want?"

Will just stared at her from the back of the plane.

"Fine." She shrugged. "I'll have the chicken."

She started to walk back towards the seating area.

"I don't eat beef," Will announced almost petulantly.

"Since when?" Holly asked, surprised.

"A few years ago, I decided that I wasn't going to eat any animal that I thought had cute eyes," he stated.

"That's strangely non-specific," she said.

"I finally realised that I couldn't go full vegetarian. It's not in me to do that, but I felt that I could at least stop eating animals like cows and sheep."

"What about pigs?"

"Nope. Nice eyes."

"Obviously, deer are out," Holly added. "Are you saying that you don't think chickens have cute eyes?"

"No," he replied. "Do you?"

"I never really gave it that much thought but now that you mention it…no, I guess they don't."

Holly put the box she'd grabbed back into the fridge and retrieved the other one.

"The chicken box is on the bottom shelf," she said as she returned to her seat.

Will watched her open the prepacked meal and felt his stomach rumble. With a loud sigh, he got to his feet and grabbed the other meal.

"Did you know that there's a bottle of your favourite Chardonnay in here?" he called to her.

"Charlene always arranges to have one ready and chilled when I'm travelling."

"Why am I not surprised?" Will mentioned. "She's probably one of the most efficient people I know."

"That she is," Holly replied.

"Do you want some?" he asked, holding up the bottle.

"Only if you join me?" she countered.

"Why do you think I brought it up?"

Will returned with his boxed meal under his arm, the bottle in one hand and two glasses in the other.

"I bet you didn't remember..." Holly started to say.

Will retrieved the corkscrew he'd found in one of the service drawers from his trouser pocket before she could finish.

"I'm not an idiot."

"I never thought that you were," Holly said.

For a brief moment their eyes met, but Holly quickly turned away and reached for the glass that Will had just filled.

There was an uncomfortable silence until they had both tucked into their food and the first glass of wine had kicked in.

"I know that you will find this hard to believe," Holly began, "but I was as horrified as you were back there. I fully expected to see something other than the dorm and cafeteria that they show visitors, but I never imagined it was going to be that bad. Those were some of the most inhumane work conditions I've ever seen."

"If you didn't expect to find something wrong, why did you want to do a second site visit?" Will asked.

Holly took a sip of wine and for a moment closed her eyes.

"Something happened when I was in Greenland that just made me feel that I needed to see one of their facilities as they really are."

"What happened over there?"

"I can't discuss it, but let's just say that I came back with a slightly different view of things. While I was away, I kept flashing back to you pleading with me to not keep my eyes closed to how Ling Chow treats his workers."

"I never thought that anything I said actually got through to you," Will said. "I'm glad that there's a little of the old Holly in there somewhere."

Their eyes met again. Holly turned her head away.

"Just because I agree with you about the way they're treating their people doesn't mean that anything's changed between us," Holly stated. "I can't afford to be that person again."

Will watched as Holly returned to her meal as if nothing had happened.

She knew that he was looking at her but refused to meet his gaze. There was something comforting about being alone with him again after so many years. It was more than that. She wished that she could curl up in his arms and feel his touch, but she knew that her success was, like so much in life, incredibly fragile. It had taken her years to reach the pinnacle of business and she couldn't risk losing that for something as trifling as falling back in love.

Who was she kidding? Falling back in love? She'd never stopped loving him for a minute. She'd just learned to lock such trivial emotions deep within her psyche.

She could see that she'd hurt him again. She hated that she still had that effect on him. She thought back to that day when she broke up with him all those years ago. They'd spent the day together in Central Park. It was idyllic. Holly could remember it as if it were yesterday. The worst part was that, while they were enjoying themselves and sharing those experiences, she was all too aware that she was about to irrevocably sever the relationship. She'd originally planned to do it one week later, but that day had been special.

Too special.

For a brief moment, as they laughed themselves silly after a fearless pigeon stole a piece of French bread right off Will's paper plate, Holly had a vision of them staying together. Of a normal life without wealth and power. Just the two of them against the world.

The idea had completely terrified her.

As they were walking out of the park and into the city's maze of concrete and asphalt, Holly steeled herself and told him that they had no future together. What had started as one of the happiest days of her life ended with the memory of Will standing stunned and alone on the sidewalk as he tried not to watch her walk away.

They didn't speak again until that day outside the conference room when MWL had bought the company that he worked for.

Holly cast a quick glance at Will and saw that he was staring out the window as the jet streaked above the clouds at over 600 miles an hour. She wanted to say something but didn't even know how to start.

Instead, she reclined her seat to the full flat position and willed herself to sleep.

They both managed to grab a few hours' sleep on the flight back but still arrived at Teterboro groggy and exhausted. Considering that they had spent thirty out of the last thirty-two hours on the jet, it wasn't surprising. They'd crossed so many time zones that their bodies were going to take days to recover.

"What are you going to do about the purchase?" Will asked as they taxied to the executive terminal.

"I'm not sure yet," she replied.

"Please tell me that you aren't just going to sweep it under the rug or use it as leverage to get more out of Ling Chow."

Holly looked across at him and stared into his eyes.

"Please trust me," she replied, her voice sounding raspy from the extreme jet lag. "That's all I can ask at the moment."

"I always have," he replied.

Holly stopped off at the office to catch up on some calls and emails that she hadn't wanted to work on in the air. Despite the whirlwind thirty-two-hour roundtrip and the ensuing exhaustion, she still managed to get home at her usual 8 pm. The first thing she did when she walked into her apartment was to open the laptop. She found the original email from *Reindeer Monthly* and wrote a reply.

She replied: "Need to speak with you ASAP".

She had no idea if the email address was active or even monitored but pressed send anyway.

At 8:30 pm on the dot, her doorbell rang. She was so anxious to speak with her father that she had completely forgotten about her scheduled dinner delivery. She knew that they would leave it out in the hall, so she didn't immediately get up to answer the door. After a few seconds, it rang a second time. She ignored it again, knowing that the delivery drivers had strict instruction to not disturb her.

She resumed working on a brand-new spreadsheet when the bell rang for the third time. Frustrated, she went to the door and angrily pulled it open.

"If I don't answer, it means I'm busy," she snapped.

"I just didn't want it to get cold. It smells so good."

It took Holly a moment to realise that her father was standing there holding a delivery bag from La Caprice. She had only ever seen him the one time and he'd been wearing the full Santa outfit. Seeing him in a beautifully tailored pinstripe suit was a shock. Then again, him appearing at her door only a few minutes after sending the email was quite astounding as well.

"How did you get here so fast?" she said.

"I didn't. You're just moving slowly." He grinned. "Are you going to ask me in?"

"Of course...sorry. I had no idea you were going to just turn up."

"I forgot to tell you when we were last together that phone calls don't work between the rift and your dimension," Santa said as he stepped into her entry hall. "With your world moving at glacial speed, I would have to wait a whole day just for you to get one word out."

"I guess that makes sense," Holly replied, still totally confused about the whole-time space issue. "You should try setting up an IP phone in the rift annex."

Her father stared back at her open-mouthed. Clearly nobody in the rift had ever thought of that.

"Anyway, this is my apartment." Holly gestured towards the living room.

"I know," her father replied. "It's where I first met you."

It took her a beat to realise that he was referring to

the cloned apartment in which she'd been given her orientation in the rift. She rolled her eyes at him and took the delivery bag from him.

"Are you hungry?" she asked. "They usually give me enough for two."

"I'm fine, but please, you go ahead. You must be starving after that trip to China."

"How do you know about that?"

He shrugged. "I know a lot about you."

"Don't be creepy," she said as she headed towards the kitchen. "I'm just going to dish up some of this so I can eat while we talk. It's because of my trip to China that I needed to speak with you. I have an idea on how to solve your problem and mine."

"I'm intrigued."

"How much money can you get your hands on? Real money that can be used in this dimension," Holly added.

"Almost limitless amounts," he replied. "Apart from the licensing that I told you about, we have a side business in the rift. Have you ever heard of something called Californium 252?"

"Can't say that I have," Holly said as she plated her meal.

"There's no reason you would have. It's an astounding little element that happens to cost 27 million dollars a gram. It is used to identify water and oil in drilling operations, it can help find gold and other precious metals. It can even detect metal fatigue in aircraft. It is a very sought-after item."

"Let me guess," Holly said. "You can mine it in the rift."

"Heavens, no. The elves like to work, but they would never spend the day in dark tunnels. Thankfully, something in the process that created the rift brought Californium to the surface. A short distance from where you visited, it's lying around right where you can see it. It's highly radioactive, but radiation has no effect on elves whatsoever, except to make them a little frisky. We sell a few hundred pounds of the stuff a year through an intermediary just so we have enough in the bank in case of emergencies."

"When you say, 'enough'?"

"In ready cash, I'd say we have about half a trillion dollars dotted amongst ten different banks."

"That's way more that we need," she answered. "Are you interested in picking up a bargain?"

"I'm interested in hearing what you have in mind."

"Let's go into the living room so I can eat while I show you some numbers. I think you'll get a kick out of what I have in mind."

"You look happier," he stated.

"That's just because my eyes are glazed over, I'm so tired," she replied as she walked past him with her plate of pork tenderloin slices, ratatouille and sautéed new potatoes.

The aroma reached Santa's nose.

"Did you say there was enough for two?"

CHAPTER
TWENTY-TWO

Six weeks later, the board of Marshall Whiteman Logistics convened for an emergency meeting in the top-floor conference room. Holly was summoned without warning to join them immediately.

She wasn't the least bit surprised. In fact, she was amazed that she hadn't heard from them last night or first thing that morning.

She took a look around her office for what she expected would be the last time. She wanted to feel some sense of imminent loss but felt nothing. She'd given everything to get to where she was, yet, faced with losing it all, she strangely felt only relief.

As she walked through her suite, her assistants gave her an encouraging smile. Charlene was surprised to see that Holly didn't seem the least bit fazed at having been summarily summoned to the board room. In fact, if she didn't know better, she could have sworn that Holly looked rather pleased with herself. It was almost as if she had a new spring in her step.

Holly walked into the conference room without knocking. The twelve board members and the chairman stopped what they were saying and waited while she took one of the guest chairs at the table.

With the exception of Bryce Marshall, the chairman and son of the founder, none of the others even looked at her. Holly had always felt that, unlike his father, who'd been a gentleman and a brilliant businessman, Bryce was vindictive, petty-minded and had always resented Holly for becoming CEO instead of him.

"Thank you joining us, Ms Hillman," Bryce said.

"I wasn't aware that I had a choice and why am I suddenly Ms Hillman? I thought we used first names in here."

"I presume you know why I called you here today?" Bryce asked coldly, ignoring her comment.

"I have a vague idea," Holly replied.

"Don't be flippant," he shouted. "You are in a great deal of trouble here. I suggest that you show us some respect."

Holly simply looked at him with a slight smile. She could see that that made him even angrier.

"I received word from Beijing last night that the Ling Chow Group are planning to pull out of the merger."

"I'm sorry to hear that," Holly responded.

"I can't believe," Bryce continued. "that you are acting so blasé about this situation considering it is entirely your fault. From what I was told, you added a caveat to the contract that all workers at their facilities were to be paid a minimum wage of what amounts to five dollars an hour in our currency. You also demanded that existing dormitories were to be demolished and new green structures would be built according to a design that you submitted for what you called humane and respectful accommodation. You even demanded that every facility give their staff a choice of healthy and freshly prepared meals which are to be available twenty-four hours a day."

He glared at her over the top of his half-moon spectacles. Holly couldn't help noticing that Bryce looked like an ill-tempered bulldog.

"Are you waiting for me to say something?" Holly asked.

"I'm waiting to hear what you have to say about the claims made by Ling Chow."

"I'd be delighted to give you my opinion, but you forgot a few items," Holly leaned back in her chair. "You forgot the part about them providing health care, dental and a gym."

"Are you out of your mind?" Bryce frothed. "Ling Chow is so successful because of his ability to shave costs. That's the reason this deal was ever approved. Their distribution and logistics operations cost them one tenth of what ours do and are twice as profitable. That's what we were buying into. Not some country club full of overpaid and overfed workers. If the Ling Chow Group did what you required of them, they would without question go out of business in six months."

"I'm sorry you feel that way, Bryce. What would you like me to do?" Holly said with faux sincerity.

"I want you to remove that ridiculous caveat and get this deal back on the table."

"I don't think I can do that, Bryce," she said, shaking her head.

"You'll do exactly as I tell you." Bryce was so angry he sent a salvo of spittle sailing out onto the polished wood table.

"I heard a few hours ago that Ling Chow has been purchased by another company," Holly advised. "Some distribution group from up north stepped in with an all-cash offer. I'm really sorry about this but, considering all the bad press about the use of child labour and the detention camp conditions, I think we dodged a bullet. I thought you'd all be delighted that I saved the company so much unpleasantness."

Holly gave Bryce her best smile.

Bryce's face turned purple.

Charlene was helping Holly place a few personal items into a cardboard box. Though she kept it to herself, she felt that it was a sad state of affairs that, after so many years at MWL, Holly could put all of her memories and personal items into as single box.

"I can't believe that you are leaving," she said, wiping a tear from her eye. "We've worked together for over eleven years."

"I know." Holly nodded. "You were my first hire when I became executive director."

"I never said anything, but I knew the moment I met you that you were going to end up running this place," Charlene said. "I could just tell that you were going to make it to the top."

Holly stopped wrapping a jade carving in tissue paper. "Are you going to stay on here?"

"I don't want to, but I don't know where else I would go. When you get to my age, finding a job isn't that easy."

"What do you mean, your age? You're only a few years older than me."

"Try twelve years older," Charlene corrected her. "Hopefully, they'll let me stay. Most of the executives here are spoiled little men with superiority complexes, but at least I'd be working. Ever since Stan died three years ago, I prefer not to have to spend any time alone. I feel like a stranger in my own house."

Will walked unannounced into Holly's office with a look of complete shock on his face.

"I'll leave you two alone," Charlene said as she left the room.

"They fired you?" Will could hardly get his words out.

"Something like that," she said as she gently placed her holly plant into the cardboard box. "They must have really wanted me gone. This is going to cost them a fortune."

"I'm sure," Will said. "Firing CEOs is never cheap. By the way, did you know that there's a security guard out in the hallway?"

"That's Bob," Holly replied cheerfully. "He's waiting to escort me out of the building."

"That's classy," he said, shaking his head. "I still don't understand why the board decided to fire you."

"It was that last condition that I added to the Ling Chow contract. The one you wrote up."

"But they approved it before it went out," Will stated.

Holly tilted her head to one side. "About that…"

"Don't tell me you didn't get it cleared by the board?

The Ling Chow purchase was going to be the biggest acquisition in the history of the company."

"I thought it best not to include them," Holly replied. "I had this weird feeling that, if I had shown it to them, they would have stopped us sending it."

Will looked at Holly as if she'd gone insane.

"But you knew full well that there was a chance that Ling Chow would pull out of the deal when he read that caveat. I always assumed that you'd covered yourself by getting the board's approval."

"That would certainly have been one way to go," she said, grinning.

"Oh my God!" Will said. "You wanted them to fire you. But how did you know for certain that Ling Chow would pull out? If that other buyer hadn't shown up with a cash offer, they might have stayed the course."

"You're probably right," she replied as she placed one last item in the box.

"No way!" Will said in an excited whisper. "You knew about the other offer too, didn't you?"

Holly shrugged.

"I still don't see how you benefit from doing something that you knew would get you fired."

"It does seem like a pretty stupid thing to do, doesn't it?" she replied.

Holly picked up the box and started for the door.

"Can I at least help you downstairs with that stuff?" Will asked.

"I don't think you should be seen anywhere near me, do you? At this exact moment I am the Antichrist as far as the board members and senior executives are concerned.

They'd fire you in a minute if they knew that you were the one who drafted the caveat."

"So, you're just going to walk away from me again?" Will asked.

"Remember what I said on the plane?" Holly replied. "Trust me. This is the right thing. You wouldn't be happy with me."

"Shouldn't that be my decision?" Will asked.

"Not when you can't see what I already know. I'm not the same person you fell in love with."

"But you could be," he insisted.

"You have to believe me when I tell you that I am doing us both a huge favour," Holly stated.

Will just shook his head in frustration. "Where will you go?" he asked.

"Home."

Holly stepped past him and walked out of her office for the last time. Will felt an almost crushing emptiness. Even though they hadn't been involved for years, seeing her at work had at least kept her close.

Holly stepped out onto 5th Avenue and saw a red Range Rover waiting for her at the kerb. Blitzen, in human form, jumped out and took the box from her as she slid into the back seat.

"How'd it go?" her father asked.

"Pretty much as we expected," Holly answered. "They basically fired me on the spot."

"How about your golden parachute?" he asked.

"They couldn't touch it. They would have had to show cause that I deliberately sabotaged the deal. I mentioned that, when the case went to court, I would show the conditions of the Ling Chow facility and explain that I was only trying to save the company from embarrassment and possible future liability. I also reminded them how such a case could easily garner a lot of interest from the media and that I doubted that Marshall Whiteman wanted to be known as the company that condoned such horrific treatment of their workers."

"How do you feel about personally destroying your own career?" he asked.

"Strangely…I feel good," she said. "I feel really good."

"I'm glad," he replied.

Holly patted him on the knee.

"You didn't have to come all the way here just to pick me up," she pointed out.

"I assumed that they would be petty and take away your car and driver."

"You assumed right," she said.

"I'll make sure to put them all on the naughty list," he offered.

Holly laughed.

"How's the Ling Chow deal going?" she asked.

"They were a bit put out that I didn't want them retaining any share of the company, but, as you'd guessed, they had heavily borrowed against the proceeds in anticipation of the Marshall Whiteman purchase. They found themselves in a desperate need of cash to pay off the creditors."

"Isn't greed wonderful?" Holly said sarcastically. "Did you look at my latest plans for the distribution operation?"

"Yes. They're amazing. I can't believe we've been wasting so much time and expense."

"It's almost as I was born with the distribution gene in my blood." She grinned.

"Do you want to go straight home, or do we need to stop somewhere?" her father asked.

"Aren't we going to the Pole?"

"I will," he replied. "You will be going home to relax and get your head around what you've just done. You've just drastically changed your life."

"When will I be moving to the rift?" Holly said.

"We need to talk about that," he answered.

"What's there to talk about? I've shown you what I can do. We talked about this when I told you about my plan for the Ling Chow contract. You can't just blow me off."

Donner, why don't you drive us around the park for a while," Santa said. "We look a bit obvious sitting here on 5th Avenue."

The SUV pulled away from the kerb. They passed St Patrick's Cathedral and continued on towards Central Park.

"As we discussed, I needed some time to think about where was best for you to live," her father said. "I've decided that it would be best for you to stay within your own dimension. There's nothing for you in the rift."

"There's you," Holly answered.

"You'll always have me, but to give up everything you know and care about would be a terrible choice."

"But it should be my choice," she shot back.

"The one thing that I never told you about when I was giving you my history was that I have lived a long but very lonely life. I'm surrounded by wonderful beings that are always there for me, but that's not the same as having a life companion. I had one once but lost her. While losing one's wife is devastating to any husband, doing so knowing that I was going to live countless lifetimes on my own was completely overwhelming."

"Even more reason for me to move up there with you," Holly stated. "We'd have each other. We're family."

"Thank you for saying that, but, without wanting to sound ungrateful, you are my daughter; you should be living your life. Besides, you are still young and have so much to give your dimension. Stay here, run my non-rift businesses and tear down that wall you've built in there."

Santa gently tapped her forehead.

"I've got nothing to stay here for," Holly said.

"You have everything to stay here for. Just open your eyes," he said. "Donner...let's drop my daughter off and get back home."

He turned back to face her.

"You can come up in a few days so that we start planning out this new venture, but for Heaven's sake... start enjoying your life again. Your world is a beautiful place. Don't waste it."

Holly walked into her apartment for the first time as an ex-employee of Marshall Whiteman Logistics. It was a strange sensation for someone who had chosen to place work above all else for almost half of her life. She put the box she'd brought home from the office on the floor in the hallway, then walked slowly from room to room, seeing them almost as if for first time.

She'd bought the co-op the moment she had been appointed CEO. It was the perfect home in the perfect building in the perfect city. She could walk to the park, though she never had the time to do so. She could walk to the museums and galleries but, again, work never gave her the time to enjoy such things. Or, at least, she never permitted such distractions to take her mind off her job.

When the unit became hers, instead of shopping for furniture and ornaments with family or friends, she'd hired one of New York's best interior designers to create what he felt was the suitable look for a woman CEO of a Fortune 400 company.

As she looked at her home with fresh eyes, she no longer felt the need to impress others. She saw that nothing about the 3,000-square-foot apartment felt like a real home. It felt like something from the pages of *Architectural Digest*, not somewhere that one could feel cosy and complete. Holly needed a place where she could be herself and relax among her own choice of furniture and decor.

The co-op was perfectly designed to be coldly aloof. Then again, that's what Holly had been for the past twenty years of her life.

As she stared out at the ten-million-dollar view, she suddenly realised that she needed to move out of there as soon as possible. She needed to live somewhere else. Somewhere where there was a trace of life. Maybe even a trace of joy.

CHAPTER
TWENTY-THREE

Two weeks later, Holly was back up at the North Pole going over the logistics schedules with her father. She was wearing her new business uniform: jeans, a T-shirt and a white cable knit sweater. Gone were her identical burgundy dresses. The Goodwill charity store employee had been surprised at the donation, but Holly had simply explained that they were from a theatre production that hadn't worked out.

It was the first week in December and Christmas was fast approaching. Thanks to Holly's reworking of the outdated staging plan and restocking hubs, it was starting to look like Santa's ability to deliver gifts to the world's children was back on track. The one area that had remained a logistical problem was eastern Asia. From eastern Russia all the way down through the Philippines and Malaysia, the existing NPMD hubs were no longer capable of managing the sheer volume of gifts needed to be prepped and readied for mid-air restocking. Thanks to Santa's purchase of the Ling Chow Group and especially their four distribution centres in that area, the vacuum was filled, and the gifts were already being shipped to those locations.

Santa had toured the ex-LCG facilities, unseen by any humans, of course, before purchasing them and had agreed with Holly on how to complete a quick retrofit just to get through Christmas. Once that was finished, they could then focus on a full-scale reworking of the buildings, the systems and the way the staff was housed and treated.

The first thing they did was to send the workers home at the company's expense while the initial work was carried out. They were told to spend time with their families and that they would still be paid their new, respectable salaries even while on a break.

Until Christmas was over and they had time to build entirely new family friendly housing, they demolished the horrific dormitories, and, at enormous expense, flew in hundreds of luxury RVs and placed them throughout each facility property. All were wired for power, water, waste and satellite TV.

By the time the staff returned in mid-November, they each had their own comfortable, safe housing only minutes from their jobs.

Holly had contacted every client who had been using LCG for their distribution and informed them that NPMD would not be honouring the previous owners' contracts. When the companies tried to renegotiate new deals, Holly advised them that all the facilities were now being used for alternative purposes.

Once Santa and Holly had reviewed all the Christmas prep and they'd signed off on everything, Holly revealed a plan she'd been working on ever since leaving Marshall Whiteman.

Holly wanted Santa to create a new company that would work solely in her dimension but with the support of NPMD when she needed it. Her plan was to use all of the distribution hubs and facilities as global emergency centres for charitable distributions. She wanted Santa's rift operation to sell a little more of their Californium supply and provide her with enough funds to keep all the centres full of clothing, food and medicine, as well as supplies so that temporary emergency housing could be assembled quickly anytime, anywhere.

Holly was sick of watching countries deal with droughts, natural disasters and wars without the funds to help the people who needed it, quickly. She wanted this new company to never have to rely on the whim of donors, rather, to always have sufficient funding to react the moment the need was there.

Santa loved the idea, not just for the obvious humanitarian reasons, but also because they could now keep their facilities fully operational all year round.

"If only I knew the right person to head up such an operation," Santa said as he scratched his beard. "It would have to be someone really smart and knowledgeable about logistics and distribution. They'd have to be compassionate and dedicated. I'd better start running some ads."

Holly didn't buy his gag for a second.

"I thought we'd call it *Santa's Helping Hand*," Holly suggested.

"That's a bit self-promoting, isn't it?" he replied.

"Absolutely." She grinned. "I think it just about says it all."

The first thing Holly did when she got back to New York and her dimension was to seek out offices for the new company. She knew what she was looking for and the most important aspect of the property was that it had to be as un-corporate-looking as possible. She wanted to find a place that had heart and soul, not some sterile steel-and-glass compound sixty floors above the ground.

After only two days, she found it. Her real estate agent had shown her dozens of "suitable" properties, but they all looked exactly like what they were. Boring office suites. It was while they were heading to yet another complex two blocks north of the Twin Towers Memorial that Holly shouted for the agent to stop the car. They'd been travelling south on Broadway when she saw a for sale sign just up Bond Street.

They walked back and stood in front of a wonderfully funky, three-storey building. It had obviously at one time been some sort of small factory. It had undoubtably been repurposed countless number of times, and in its latest reincarnation was a discount paint store that had failed and was going out of business. The sign said that the entire building was for sale with 14,000 square feet of space. They walked into the store and saw that it was quite unique. It had high ceilings with iron girders running east to west, presumably supporting the next floor.

Steel supports, made to look like Doric columns, rose from a rough concrete floor to the beams above. The walls were brick and looked to be original.

"We need to keep going if we're going to make the next appointment," the agent said. Her face scrunched in total distain for the property. It was obvious that she could see no redeeming features for the space.

"We don't need to see anything else," Holly said, beaming. "This will be our head office."

"But it's doesn't look anything like a corporate headquarters," the agent gasped.

"I know," Holly said. "Can I leave you to contact the sellers and make an offer? You have all our financial details."

"Don't you want to be part of the negotiations?"

"No. Not remotely," Holly said. "Try to get us the best deal you can. Just make sure you get it. I want to start moving in, in two weeks."

"But that's almost Christmas," the agent bleated.

"Exactly," Holly confirmed as she walked out of the store.

Holly had never been as busy at any point in her life as those few weeks leading up to Christmas. The building purchase had gone through and an architect was almost finished with plans to turn the space into exactly what Holly had hoped to find. It was going to be open plan but with a welcoming and positive feel. The two upper floors were being made into offices for the teams that would be ordering and tracking all the items that Santa's Helping Hand would be shipping to their distribution hubs.

Holly had already been able to get builders to convert one corner of the downstairs area into temporary offices for her and her new director of operations.

Charlene had been overcome when Holly had offered her the job. She had at first pushed back, saying that she had no experience with such important and critical responsibilities. Holly pointed out that managing her office at Marshall Whiteman was much harder and more stressful that what she'd be doing at SHH.

On the day that Charlene started work, Holly looked on as her ex-assistant arranged her desk exactly as she'd had it at MWL. She even placed her oversized snow globe, with its entombed sleigh and reindeer, in the place of honour in front of her computer. On her second day there, Charlene had asked if she could bring a few of her other Christmas items from home as she'd done at MWL during the lead-up to the holidays.

Charlene's cubicle Christmas decor had been a tradition. Despite her usual precise and professional demeanour, Charlene turned her stark work area into a winter wonderland over the holidays. Some executives at MWL had even complained about her decorations, stating that they were unsuitable and unprofessional in the workplace. Holly had stepped in and suggested that the detractors must surely have had better things to do with their time than complain about one employee's enthusiasm for Christmas.

Holly of course told her to make her new office as festive as she liked.

Holly's other great find was her new home. She'd found a tiny two-storey house on West 4th Street, in the Village. It was a third the size of her co-op but had a hundred times the charm. She planned on choosing the decor and furniture herself this time and make it into a real home. Her home.

Even before her condo was even sold, Holly began bringing over a few boxes at a time to her new abode.

She had just carried a box of bedding up to the only bedroom when the doorbell rang.

"Will," she said, astonished to see him on her doorstep. "What are you doing here?"

"That's a nice greeting," he replied. "I haven't heard a word from you since you left Marshall Whiteman."

"I've been kind of busy."

"I can see that," Will said as he peered past her into the house. "You got rid of the 007 villain lair?"

"It wasn't that bad," she replied.

"That's not what I heard from the honoured few who had seen it," he commented.

"They just didn't understand architecture," she fired back.

"Do I at least get to see the new digs?" he asked.

"Oh, sorry," she said, opening the door fully so he could squeeze by.

Will stepped into her home and immediately loved the place. It was funky, yet classy and fun. The grand tour took only two minutes.

"I love it," It's just what I'd always thought…"

Will stopped himself before finishing the thought.

"You'd always thought what?" Holly probed.

"Nothing. It's stupid."

"Finish what you were going to say," Holly insisted.

"I was going to say that this is exactly the sort of place that I'd hoped you and I would end up living in, back when…you know."

Holly took his hands in hers.

"I know what you mean, and I really wish that things could have worked out for us."

"They still can," he suggested, trying to sound light-hearted.

"No, they can't," Holly insisted. "You've heard the Thomas Wolfe expression that you can never go back home again? Well, that also applies to you and me."

"What, that we can't ever go home again?" Will countered. "I wasn't aware that we'd ever had a home."

"You know what I mean," Holly replied.

"I actually don't. What we had was special and I know that we could get it back if we tried. I mean, look at you. You've given up the corporate world and found a real home. These are all huge changes for you. The old Holly is trying to fight her way back to the surface."

"There is no old Holly, just the latest version of her," she explained.

"I don't believe that, and you know what? I don't think that do either. You're just stuck in a character that you created."

Holly looked into his eyes, and for a brief moment wanted to pull him close and feel his arms around her.

"What are you doing here on a workday?" she asked, changing the subject. "Plus, what's with the jeans and sweater look?"

"I could say the same thing," he joked as he looked down at her outfit. "I quit the company two days after you left. I hated the place. If you hadn't been there, I would have done it years ago."

"Oh, Will," Holly said, shaking her head. "I'm so sorry."

"Without you being there, MWL just became what I guess it always was. A cold, heartless money-making machine."

"I can't disagree with you about MWL," Holly said. "Maybe it's best for both of us that we won't be seeing each other at work anymore."

"You don't mean that," he replied.

"We can't just start back up from where we left off. That was a lifetime ago."

"Then let's start afresh," Will suggested.

"I can't. There's too much going on in my life right now."

Will was about to respond when Holly cut him off. "I'm sorry but I've got to get over to my new offices. My backer is coming by this afternoon to check out the place."

"I'll get going, then," he said. "I just wanted to make sure you were alright."

"I'm fine." she nodded. "Really."

Will gave her a forced smile and stepped back onto the street. Holly watched as he walked along 4th Street, then turned around a corner. She leaned against her front door frame and closed her eyes. Her heart was beating too fast, and she could feel tears forming in her eyes. She chewed her bottom lip as she realised that that may well have been the last time she would ever see him.

Holly had wanted to tell him that the moment she'd first stepped into her new home, she thought exactly the same thing – and briefly imagined how happy they could have been, living in the tiny house, together.

Holly knew that the only thing that was keeping them apart was her own overdriven sense of emotional self-preservation.

The only reason that existed for her not letting Will back into her life – her personal life, was that she was scared. No – she was terrified. She was frightened about what would happen if they did try to make it work and it failed. It was easier for her to push him away. That way, she was guaranteed to not be hurt.

She shook away such unproductive thoughts and carried on unpacking one of the boxes.

Her Village house was only a short walk to work. It only took her ten minutes, during which time she got to enjoy seeing the mass of people all busily getting on with their lives. When she'd been at MWL, between her co-op, her chauffeured ride and her office in the clouds, she had rarely felt connected with the city's population. She regretted that now.

Holly walked into the headquarters of SHH and heard Charlene singing "Silent Night" to herself in her temp office. Holly smiled as she walked to the back of the building. Suddenly, she heard another voice join in with Charlene's singing. It was male and low, almost operatic. Holly stepped into the doorway and was shocked to see her father helping Charlene decorate a huge Christmas tree.

"You're early," Holly said.

Santa stopped singing.

"You have a wonderful father," Charlene said. "I love the fact that he put on the whole Santa outfit just to visit."

"Yeah," Holly said raising her eyebrows to him. "That was wonderful of you."

"What can I say?" he replied. "Sometimes, you just have to go a little crazy."

"I told him that that's exactly how I feel at this time of year," Charlene gushed.

"May I borrow him for a while?" Holly asked while still glaring at her father. "We have some plans and schedules to look at."

"Of course you can," Charlene replied.

As her father started for the door, he had a thought and turned back to Charlene."

"Just remember…the weather outside is frightful."

Charlene giggled. "But the fire is so delightful."

"Good grief," Holly said under her breath as she steered him out of the room.

CHAPTER
TWENTY-FOUR

Suddenly, it was Christmas Eve. Holly had completed her move into her new home and signed over the deed to the buyer of her old co-op. Holly met him at the title company and couldn't help feeling that he and the apartment were a perfect match. He was in his mid-thirties, wore a grey Brioni suit, had slicked-back hair and was wearing Ferragamo loafers without socks. She could almost smell the ambitious greed coming off him in waves.

Then again, she'd been him ten years ago.

Holly had hoped that Charlene would have been able to stop by the new offices for an eggnog at some point over the holidays, but she'd had a sudden emergency and couldn't come by until after Christmas.

Most people who found themselves alone at that time of year, settle into a sad loneliness that ran from December 20th to January 2nd. Holly had never succumbed to such emotions. She used to work through Christmas Eve and even through the big day itself. She could never understand why people who were alone all year suddenly got morose just because of a few dates on the calendar. This year was different. It wasn't that Holly felt depressed or saddened by Christmas; it was just that for the first time in ages she felt alone.

She'd wanted to be up in the control centre within the rift, but Santa had refused to let her work during that particular holiday. Holly had promised to just observe and not say a word, but they both knew that such behaviour was literally not in her DNA. He told her that, for once, she was to enjoy Christmas without stress.

"Watch some of the Christmas movies," he suggested. "*Miracle on 34th Street* and *It's a Wonderful Life* are my favourites, but you should find your own."

In a moment of peevishness, Holly had replied, "How about *Bad Santa*?"

He'd laughed. "I personally can't stand it, but the elves love it. They start watching it in November and mimic scenes from it all the way through mid-January."

Holly had watched his two recommendations as well as a number of other, newer films. Not that she'd admit it to anyone, but she had enjoyed them all and even cried at some of the endings.

Holly poured herself her second glass of eggnog and Kahlua and sat watching her Christmas tree lights flicker from a shimmering gold to a forest green. She'd never had a Christmas tree in her life. Her first adoptive parents thought they were sacrilegious, and her hippy ones thought that chopping down a living trees just to celebrate a pagan festival was a complete abomination.

She had been going to keep up her tradition of not having a tree at all, but two days earlier, a seven-foot spruce arrived on her doorstep complete with a large box of decorations and lights. Having no idea how to decorate a tree, she had to go on Google so she could watch a couple of how-to videos. She'd turned on her new Bose Wave and found a station playing nothing but Christmas songs.

It took her almost three hours to decorate the tree. She'd started over twice as she wasn't happy with how it was looking. Now, as she sat back and admired her handiwork, she felt a sense of pride but also a feeling of joy. Holly had no idea where that emotion could come from just by looking at a tree, but it had started as she untied the Christmas tree and had steadily grown throughout the day.

She glanced over at her mantle clock sitting next to the plant she'd received in Greenland and saw that it was almost eight o'clock. Santa would have completed almost two thirds of his deliveries. She hoped her new schedule had worked out as well as they'd planned.

Holly's doorbell rang. It was her dinner. She'd cancelled the fancy nightly delivery from La Caprice and had even started to cook for herself, but on Christmas Eve she couldn't bear the idea of trying to cook something just for one. She'd decided to use her food app and chose a restaurant in Chinatown that was near the office and had great reviews on the delivery site.

Holly hadn't eaten Chinese food since she and Will had splurged on a full dim sum feast in China Town over twenty years earlier. The food had been delicious and, back then, very adventurous for their young palates. She remembered how neither of them had been able to eat the steamed chicken feet. They were just too real.

That had been the night before the picnic in the park and the end of their relationship.

Holly's doorbell rang only a few seconds after her phone app notified her that her food was about to arrive. She opened the front door and was surprised to see a young man on a racing bike holding out her bag of food. Holly wasn't sure what she'd expected, maybe an elderly and wise-looking Chinaman. Instead, she got Ted from Brooklyn.

She quickly scanned the contents of the bag and saw that her egg rolls were missing. She pointed out the egregious error to Ted, expecting him to make some lame excuse so he wouldn't have to return again, but Ted was sincerely apologetic and promised to be back within ten minutes with the missing appetisers. She carried her food into the kitchen and as she started to remove each carton from the bag she was stunned at how much food they'd given her, considering how restrained she been with her ordering.

She wanted to wait for the eggrolls to arrive, but couldn't resist the aroma, which was almost making her drool. Holly curled up on her new sofa, switched on her TV and started watching *The Santa Clause* as she ate chicken low mein right out of the box. She was on her third mouthful when the doorbell rang again. She was pleasantly surprised at how quickly Ted had managed to return with her missing items.

"That was fast. I thought…" Holly said.

Her father, Santa, was standing grinning at her as he almost filled her door frame.

"What are you doing here?" she asked. "You don't have time to stop here tonight. You should be delivering gifts."

"I am delivering gifts," he replied. "My people inform me that, despite a shaky start to the year, you ended up on the 'nice' list."

"Don't be silly," Holly said, laughing. "You didn't have to stop here tonight."

"Actually, I think that this is one of the most important stops I'll make this year. You're my daughter and I believe that I have the one gift that you seem unable to give yourself."

"That's ridiculous," Holly insisted. "If there was something I wanted that badly, I would have bought it myself."

"If that were true, I wouldn't need to be here tonight," Santa whispered.

Her father then held out a single Chinese food take-out carton.

"You came all the way here just to bring me my egg rolls?"

"Not just the egg rolls," he replied. "I thought you needed something else to go with your meal."

Santa stepped aside, revealing Will standing behind him.

Holly felt tears form in her eyes as she looked at him. He looked cold and confused and, somewhat out of character, was wearing a brightly coloured Christmas sweater with a bright red reindeer emblazoned on the front.

"Your dad is Santa Claus," Will stated as if in a daze.

"Dad, you didn't give him your special milk and cookies, did you?" Holly asked.

"Maybe just enough to calm him down a little. When the SUV turned into the sleigh, he seemed a little shocked."

"Most people would be," Holly remarked. "Where is the sleigh?"

Holly craned her neck out the door and saw the red Range Rover double-parked a few houses down the street. She waved at Donner and Blitzen, who were waving back at her through the windscreen.

"I took him for a little ride up north before bringing him here. I felt he might need to get a quick glimpse of the bigger picture before accepting that I wasn't just kidnapping him."

"Which you did, by the way," Holly remarked.

"Are you okay?" Holly asked Will.

"I am now. I was a little worried for a moment that I was being abducted by aliens, but now that I know that it was just your dad…"

"You'd better come in. I have some Chinese food on the go, if you're interested," Holly offered almost shyly.

"Do you have enough?" he asked. "I could go down the street and get some more."

"She has plenty," Santa said knowingly. "I believe they delivered enough for two."

"You're too much," Holly said as she hugged her father.

"Do you like your gift?" he asked.

Holly started to cry.

"It's the best gift I've ever had," Holly replied as she took Will's hand and pulled him into her home.

As she closed the door, she nodded at her father and mouthed, "Thank you."

He gave her a wink, then headed over to the SUV.

"You can be a real softy sometimes," Donner said as Santa climbed in the back.

"Don't tell the elves," he replied. "I'll have a mutiny on my hands in no time. Let's get back to the rift so I can pick up my new helper."

CHAPTER
TWENTY-FIVE

With the kids long ago grown up and moved out, Sofia and Tony didn't have to wake up early on Christmas Day anymore. There was no patter of feet or begging faces to motivate their parents up and into the living room.

It had been a tough road, but now things were just fine. They were still living in the same apartment, but their super had at least given the walls a coat of paint in the autumn and even fixed the broken tap in the bathroom.

Mia was living out in Arizona, selling real estate and doing pretty well at it. Joey had his own wife and kids and was teaching geography at a nice little school in New Jersey.

Ever since Quicky Lube had fired Tony all those years ago, he'd had trouble finding and keeping steady employment. Without that degree that he'd never earned, and that run-in with the police over that little girl they found under their tree, real jobs had been hard to come by. Even though the police had finally accepted that he was probably innocent, they were never able to find out where the little girl had come from. They wanted to use the media to show her face and get some call-ins, but the DA's office decided that, if the child was in some sort of danger, advertising where she was wouldn't have been the most prudent thing to do.

When they'd tried to gently coax any information out of the young girl, she just kept saying that she wanted her papa, but couldn't describe him or tell them where she was from. Their only clue had been when one of the officers brought his new coffee mug to work that his wife had given him for Christmas. The sides of the mug were adorned with mug-shots of Santa Claus. Under the photos were the words: WANTED FOR FAILING TO PROVIDE A DECENT PRESENT AT CHRISTMAS.

The little girl jumped off her chair and began pointing at the mug.

"Papa!" she squealed.

"Great," one of the officers said sarcastically. "We finally got our first lead. We'd better get a car up to the North Pole ASAP."

They ended up keeping Tony in jail for three weeks before releasing him due to a lack of evidence. When Tony was finally allowed to return home and their kids were returned back them, the police never offered so much as an apology. Even though the charges had been dropped, Quicky Lube's corporate office had deemed that Tony was not a good fit for their brand and, if word got out that they were employing a suspected child kidnapper, all the negative media exposure would do irreparable damage to their business.

Tony was currently working a twenty-hour week for an industrial cleaning company, but that on its own didn't bring in enough to keep food on the table.

Sofia had somehow put herself through night trade school, and learned how to be a computer repair tech. She worked for one of the big-box electrical stores and was on call seven days a week to drive one of their brightly coloured Fiats to fix computers in customers' homes.

The job paid a decent enough living wage but there was never much left over for any little extras or to put away anything for a rainy day.

As the grey light of another depressing Newark morning bled through their cheap curtains, Sofia swung her legs out of bed.

"Come on, old man. Let's go see what Santa brought us," she joked.

Santa had of course, not visited since Mia and Joey stopped believing in him all those years ago. Sofia and Tony now pretty much knew exactly what was under their ten-year-old artificial tree. They had, after all, been together at the dollar store when they bought each other their gifts. Still, they donned their dressing gowns and slippers and padded down the hall to the living room.

Everything was exactly as they'd left it when they went to bed the previous night, with the exception of a cream-coloured envelope leaning between a glass of milk and a plate of cookies on the coffee table.

"That's cute, hon," Sofia said.

"Huh?" Tony mumbled sleepily. "I didn't do that. Are you saying you didn't do that?"

The two approached the table as if the envelope were going to bite.

Tony gingerly picked it up and tried to see through the heavily bonded paper without success.

"Just open it," Sofia said.

Tony carefully dug his finger under the flap and slid it across. He pried open the envelope and removed a folded piece of paper.

He unfolded it and started to read it to himself.

"What's it say?" she said, nudging him.

"It says, 'Sorry about all the trouble I put you through. I hope this helps.' Then at the bottom it says, 'You may want to eat a cookie and have some milk if you need to calm down.'"

Tony, concerned about anything unexpected appearing at Christmas, looked at the back of the piece of paper, then checked the envelope. Tucked in the bottom was a single scratch card for something called the North Pole Lottery. It had dancing reindeer on the front and three foil squares near the bottom.

Sofia gave him an angry, questioning glare.

"I didn't buy this. I know what we agreed to. I haven't bought any of these in years."

"If not you, then who? It wasn't me!" Sofia declared, her hands on her broad hips. "Well, it's here now, so scratch the damn thing!"

Tony found a quarter on the table and scratched the first foil square. Under it was a drawing of a sleigh. He scratched the next one and got another sleigh.

"I got two sleighs," he said proudly.

"That ain't gonna mean much unless you get the third one."

Tony scratched the third square very slowly. He finally uncovered enough to make out the third red sleigh.

"I got it. I got three red sleighs."

"Uh huh," Sofia said, looking unimpressed. "So, what did we win? I'm not going to get all excited for five dollars."

Tony turned the card over and saw rows of tiny print that were too small for him to read. He tried squinting but that didn't help.

"Give me that," she said, grabbing it from him.

Sofia picked up the magnifying glass that she used for her crossword puzzles and started reading.

"It's all a bunch of mumbo jumbo about winnings being automatically deposited in our account and that all monies have already had the tax deducted."

"I don't care about all that," Tony scolded. "What the heck did we win?"

"Here it is, down at the bottom. Three elves is ten dollars; three bunches of mistletoe is twenty-five dollars."

"Now it's getting interesting," Tony said.

"Three Christmas trees is fifty dollars, and three sleighs is…what does this say?" She adjusted the magnifier to get a better look. "The print's even smaller. It says that three sleights is…darn, it's hard to see. I think it's five hundred dollars."

"Wow." Tony clapped his hands.

"No wait, there's more zeros," she said as she squinted harder. "There's six of them."

"Six of what?" Tony cried out.

"Six…zeros," Sofia said as she slowly sat herself down on the couch.

"We won six zeros? What the heck does that mean?"

"No, honey. We won six zeros after the five."

"Now you're just talking nonsense. What do you mean six zeros after a five?"

"It says here that we just won five million dollars."

"Well, that isn't possible, so the thing must be some kinda gag gift," Tony declared. "You know what? That's a mean trick to play on someone at Christmas. I've half a mind to find out who sent this and give them an earful."

Their phone ringing interrupted his rant.

Sofia picked it up.

"Uh huh," she said. "Uh huh. Uh huh. How much? Okay. Thank you."

She disconnected the call and reached for a cookie.

"What was that about?" Tony asked.

"That was the main clearance centre for our bank. The manager there apologised for calling us on Christmas Day but, because of the nature of the deposit, wanted to let us know that the funds we were expecting have just been received and will show up in our account tomorrow."

"What funds?" Tony managed to ask in barely more than a whisper.

"The five million dollars."

Tony plopped down next to her. They stared at each other for a good few seconds, then Tony reached across her for the other cookie.

CHAPTER
TWENTY-SIX

One of Holly's suggestions before the Christmas rush had been for a small communications area to be set up in the rift annex. The plan was for them to test out communications between Holly and others in her dimension rather than require an in-person visit every time Santa and Holly wanted to talk.

Despite the annex still having some degree of the rift's time lag issue, they found that WhatsApp actually worked pretty well in the video mode. Zoom wasn't bad but occasionally there was an audio lag-loop which resulted in a deafening burst of feedback, making it impossible to complete the video call. Unfortunately, they could hardly call customer service to help them out with an interdimensional rift communication problem.

Holly let her father have some peace and quiet on Christmas Day so he could recover from his Christmas Eve delivery marathon. She also wanted the time to do something personal for a change.

On the morning after Christmas, she opened her phone app and video-called Santa. It took a few minutes to get him to come from the rift into the annex but that was a small price to pay for their new interdimensional communication link.

"How did it go?" Holly asked as she studied her father's face for any sign of the exhaustion he must have been feeling.

"Spectacularly well," he replied. "We finished slightly ahead of schedule for the first time ever."

Holly noticed that her father did look a little tired but, at the same time, exceedingly happy.

"How wonderful. Well done," she said.

"No," Santa said. "Well done you. It was mainly your system that made it work so well."

"Mainly?" Holly asked with a cheeky smile.

"I tried out something a little different this year," Santa explained. "I had a helper in the sleigh. Having the gift sack prepped before every home drop freed me up to focus on the entry and departure."

"Which of the elves did you get to help you?" Holly asked.

"Oh, it wasn't an elf," Santa replied. "You know they get terribly air sick. That would have been a nightmare."

"Then who did you get to help?"

At that moment, a hand holding a mug of hot chocolate entered the shot. It placed the steaming brew in front of Santa, who gave someone off camera a silent thank you.

"Who's that, Dad?" Holly asked.

"Is that Holly?" Charlene's unmistakeable voice said as she scooted Santa over so she could see the screen.

"Charlene?" Holly gasped. "What the heck are you doing up there? I thought you had an emergency?"

"I did," she replied, giggling. "I had to get up to the North Pole as fast as possible."

"But...how...I don't understand," Holly stammered.

"Oh, for Heaven's sake child," Santa joined in. "Do we really have to spell it out?"

"You mean...you and Charlene? You're...together?" Holly managed to ask.

"Almost since that day we met at the new office," Charlene replied as she kissed Santa's whiskery cheek.

"What can I say?" Santa kissed her back. "I never believed in soul mates before, but, thanks to you, I finally met mine. Speaking of which, where's Will?"

"He's out getting us coffee."

"Did he decide yet on my offer?" he asked.

"I should let him tell you," Holly answered. "Wait; I hear the front door."

"You wouldn't believe the queue at the coffee place," Will said as he walked into the tiny dining room.

"I'm talking to my dad...and Charlene," Holly advised him.

"I thought you were going to call the North Pole?" Will asked as he sat next to Holly. "Hi, Charlene."

"Hi, Will," Charlene said coyly.

It took Will a second to realise what he was looking at on the iPad.

"You're up there?" he said.

"I sure am," she replied holding up her left hand. A beautiful five-carat, single-stone, purple diamond ring was on her ring finger.

Both Holly's and Will's mouths dropped open.

"What a gorgeous diamond," Holly said, impressed. "Where did you get it?"

"I forgot to mention that, when we collect the Californium, we first have to clear the ground of all the diamonds that cover the surface," her father explained. "It seems that, when the rift formed billions of years ago, planets in the different dimensions were torn apart. The only thing that survived the devastation were diamonds that literally fell over this entire area. One of our biggest problems is to not slip and fall on them they're so plentiful."

"But the colour…"

"That's just one shade. The elves once counted that there were over 800 different diamond colours here. Lucky for us, not one of those colours exists in your dimension. It makes them very valuable."

"Well, Charlene," Holly said. "I couldn't be more delighted. Surprised, but delighted."

"I hope you will both be available to come up here in just over two of your weeks?" her father asked. "It will be a simple ceremony, but it would be nice to have you both up here to share it with us. In fact, while you're here and we'll have a preacher and all…" Santa quipped.

"There's no way I would ever even consider having a double wedding with my father, thank you very much," Holly declared as Will grinned next to her.

"So, Will," Santa said, changing the subject. "You've had a couple of days to think about it. What's your answer? Are you going to be the head of Santa's Helping Hand's legal department or what?"

"It's a great offer, Santa, and a guy would have to be an idiot to turn you down…"

"That's great news," Santa boomed.

"BUT…" Will continued. "I don't think I would feel comfortable working for my wife," Will advised with a straight face.

Holly and Will held out their left hands. Each had a simple gold band on their ring fingers.

"But…how…when…?" her father stammered. "You only got back together on Christmas Eve."

"It was something that should have happened twenty years ago. You showed me that," Holly explained.

"But where did you find to get married on Christmas Day?" Santa asked.

"We made a quick trip to Greenland," she said with a wave of her hand. "Gunnar was only too pleased to officiate at the service, or had you forgotten that your friend was a minister?"

"I can't even find the right words to tell you how happy I am that you finally found your heart again," he said, sniffling.

"Same goes to you too, Dad," Holly said as she wiped "something" from her eye.

Santa had to brush away a few tears as well, but pretended he was just scratching his face.

"Will," Charlene said. "I think we found ourselves a couple of softies, don't you?"

"Like father, like daughter," Will replied.

"Wait a minute!" Holly almost shouted. "Dad! I just realised! You stole my director of operations!"

"Yeah," he smiled as he nodded his head. "I guess I did."

Holly had the honour of walking her father down the aisle, which was covered by the most beautiful carpeting Holly had ever seen. It looked to have been woven from real gold thread, yet was soft and gentle underfoot. The ceremony was being held in one of the 5D relativity rooms. It was a clone of St Andrew's Church in Alfriston, in the UK. Charlene had visited it as a child and had never forgotten its simplicity and beauty. Santa had originally wanted to invite every being in the rift to attend his wedding and was planning to clone one of earth's bigger cathedrals but Holly and Charlene both convinced him that a smaller service would be more intimate and romantic and that, if he wanted to go completely over the top, he could do so for the reception.

They decided on only having one hundred and fifty guests at the service. Twenty were by direct invite but the other one hundred and thirty invitations, so as to be completely fair to all inhabitants, were picked at a public drawing two days previously.

Because Charlene had no friends or family to witness her big day, Blitzen, in human form, gave her away and Holly acted as her bridesmaid.

Holly was not surprised to see Gunnar step up in front of the attendees to perform the service. His brother Petar was holding hands with Donner who'd also taken human form for the festivities.

"Ladies, gentlemen, elves and all other species, please take your seats if you are physically able, or stand at the sides if needed," Gunnar began. "We are gathered here today to bring together…"

Holly had never realised just how sentimental the elves could be. There were about a hundred of them in the chapel and they began crying so loudly that she hardly heard another word of the service until the vows, when they finally managed to control themselves for a few minutes.

Her father was immaculately dressed in a black suit with a red tie adorned with little Christmas trees.

"Charlene," he said as he took her hands in his, "I never thought I would find love again. Not here or in any other dimension. Yet, less than a month ago, as I walked into that converted paint store, I heard you singing 'All I Want for Christmas Is You', from inside your office and felt an electric shock go through my whole body. When I stepped into that doorway, I felt something I didn't believe was still in me. I felt child-like hope and excitement.

"Charlene, you are my Christmas present. You have given a silly old man something to wake up for every morning. You have thawed a long-frozen heart and brought light back into my soul. I had forgotten what it feels like to be genuinely in love again. I never want to go a minute without such a feeling ever again."

Charlene had to wipe an errant tear away before beginning.

"Otto, when you stepped into my doorway, I somehow knew instantly that you were the actual Santa Claus. The one who brings glorious happiness to billions of people every year. I also saw something else that day. I saw the man beneath the Santa veneer. A kind and caring man. A man who has spent his life ensuring that he brought a little joy into people lives. I knew from the first moment that I saw you that we would be together.

"Ever since I lost my first husband, I assumed that I'd had my chance at love and would end my days alone as so many do. I never imagined for one moment that I would be given a second opportunity to love another person. When you explained to me that by moving here to the rift, I would be giving up everything I loved back in my dimension, I told you then and I'm telling you now: everything I love, everything I care for, everything I need, is standing right in front of me."

That was the last part of the service that Holly heard. The elves didn't just resume their crying; they veritably wailed.

It didn't matter.

She knew the gist of what was being said. She could also see the joy on the faces of Charlene and her father.

She'd never seen two people look happier.

Santa's wedding reception took place in the terminal bubble where Holly had initially been alarmed at seeing the actual tear in the rift high above her, through the glass dome. The elves had, as usual, gone completely over the top and had spread miles of white, almost transparent silk over the entire inside of the glass bowl. They'd up-lit the material from a hundred different spotlights and had also created a latticework of soft golden twinkle bulbs that were suspended across the entire space only a few above everyone's head.

Dozens of massive tables draped in cream-coloured linen were laden with an astonishing assortment of food, some recognisable by those from earth's dimension, some not. Other tables were piled high with champagne, wines (both earth-brewed and local to various other worlds), beer, as well as oat ale which was being served (with or without alcohol) for the Korks, spiced rum cocoa for the elves and a strange black molasses-like concoction for the Wooblegangers. There must have been close to 5,000 guests in the bubble. They all seemed to be having a great time.

Will was initially a little freaked out over the Korks. Some of them had stayed in their normal reindeer form, while others had been sampling the alcoholic oat ale and were showing off to their friends by seeing who could change shape the fastest and the most often. It wasn't just that they were changing; it was what they were changing into that was discombobulating for him. Some were easy to recognise, like Santa or the elves, but some were totally alien and, in a few cases, very scary-looking. Also watching the Korks, a glass of ale in his hand, was Minik, the bartender from the hotel in Nuuk. Holly waved at him, trying to get his attention.

"Who's that?" Will asked.

"That's one of the people responsible for my being here."

They both then watched Minik put his glass on the floor, move a few feet away and transform back into his real shape. It turned out that Minik was a Kork and had only transferred into the Minik form so that he could interface with Holly back at the bar in Nuuk.

The grand finale of the party was when the tables and guests were moved to the sides of the bubble and close to a thousand elves gathered in the centre of the chamber. As one, they removed their woollen hats and allowed their golden hair to rise above them.

As Holly looked on in sheer wonder, they slowly spread out into a large oval that took up most of the floor space.

Their hair gracefully floated down and loosely knotted with that of the nearest elves. Every elf was then connected to the others. As one, they slowly started to rotate. Their golden hair began to glow and sparkle. The elves all began to hum a low bass tone that reverberated through the entire space. Suddenly the white linen that had shielded the dome from view vanished in less than a second. In its place was a massive mirror that covered the entire interior of the bowl, fifty feet in the air above the guests.

It reflected perfectly what the elves were doing on the floor. Holly gasped and grabbed Will's hand as she saw that they had recreated the most beautiful vision of a galaxy that was slowly rotating on its axis.

"That's impossible," Will said, his voice choked with emotion.

"If there's one thing that I've learned recently," Holly replied. "it's that, as long as we have hope, imagination and free will; nothing is impossible."

EPILOGUE

The chartered jet touched down at Weng Chi airstrip at eight forty-seven in the morning, local time. There was no luxurious vehicle waiting for them on the tarmac. Only a bright red and green golf cart with the Santa's Helping Hand logo parked off to the side in its own little carport. Holly unplugged it from the terminal wall where it had been charging, and the two climbed into it. With her baby bump starting to show, Holly had taken to wearing looser clothing, which she now had to tuck underneath herself while perched in the golf cart.

The new road that had been laid earlier in the year was blessedly bump and rut free. It was hot out and they could both feel the humidity as it clung to them. They had both already visited the complex a number of times since the purchase, but this was the first time they'd experienced it in July.

"I can't wait to see the new building in operation," Will said as he mopped his forehead with his shirt sleeve.

"Me too," Holly agreed. "I hope the workers like their new homes."

"How could they not? I'd move here in a minute," Will added.

"Are you glad you changed your mind about not working for me?" Holly asked.

"I didn't," Will answered. "I consult for you. That's completely different to working for you."

"Is it, though?" Holly asked with a cheeky grin.

They passed by the main distribution facility and kept going until they reached the colourful wall and the arched entry to the residential areas. This had previously been the deceptively cheerful facade that led to the horrific dormitories and feeding area. Holly parked against the wall, then took Will's hand as they walked through.

Holly had seen the new residential park halfway through construction. Will had only seen the design drawings. Neither had seen the final thing until then. Gone were the drab grey monstrosities as well as the cheaply made wooden structures. Now, a gently sloping lawn spread out before them. On either side, hundreds of brightly painted townhouses were dotted throughout.

It had been transformed into looking like an upmarket golf course estate rather than housing for workers.

In the middle of the twenty-acre park was the main recreation and cafeteria building. They walked in and roamed around the immaculate and carefully designed structure. On the ground floor was the cafeteria that was open 24/7 and served a wide selection of foods from all areas of China, as well as some of the people's favourite imports like pizza and burgers. At the far end of the room, there was an area just for beverages which included a small, franchised Starbucks counter. There were scores of workers and family members eating, drinking and enjoying this new freeing experience.

They left by a side door and found themselves in a hallway. At one end was the entrance to the gym and basketball court and on the other side was a large auditorium which the workers could use for meetings, performances or to watch movies on the huge flat-screen TV.

They took the stairs and went up to the next floor. This had been Will's idea and the two of them couldn't wait to see what it looked like. Because the facility was located almost a hundred miles from the nearest town and five hundred from the nearest city, the workers rarely got a chance to go shopping, something they were able to do now that they actually had money to spend.

Will had overseen the design and planning for an indoor mall that took up the entire top of the building. They could buy clothing, electronics, books, magazines, jewellery – you name it. At the far end was a small supermarket with everything they could need if they wanted to cook and eat in their own homes.

It was gorgeous. It was modern yet cleverly had hints and traces of Chinese art and history in its design and decoration. Even as early as nine in the morning, there were dozens of people shopping. This was the only area in the complex where the workers could spend their money but, even here, the prices were incredibly low thanks to SHH subsidising the costs.

When Holly had carried out her unannounced tour of the facility when it was owned by Ling Chow, the workers hardly even glanced at her. They kept their heads down and their eyes intentionally diverted. Now, they all stared openly at her and Will. They must have known who they were as many ran up to the pair, their eyes misted over, and took their hands and bowed in an open show of respect for what they'd done. Holly couldn't help noticing that they all looked much healthier and seemed to radiate a sense of self-worth.

One worker was so excited to see Holly that he grabbed her and Will by the arm and led them outside and walked them to his home. He opened the front door and held it so that his guests could enter. The man spoke no English and neither Will nor Holly spoke Chinese, so conversation was carried out by a mix of facial and hand gestures.

Despite the language barrier, Will and Holly understood how proud the man was of his home and that his name was Hon Lu. In the small garden at the back of the townhouse they met Lila, Hon's wife, who was hanging laundry up on a clothesline. She joined her husband in showing the couple around every room of their home. It was modest but clean and new. They had supplemented the furniture that came with the house by adding a few ornaments and pictures.

At one point Holly couldn't help but flash back to the conditions she'd seen within the compound only ten months earlier.

Holly and Will walked back through the archway, deeply satisfied at what they'd seen.

They walked to the main distribution building and

were met at the front entrance by the new general manager, Wu Chiang. He greeted them warmly and seemed almost excited at the chance to show the guests his operation. Gone was the mistrust and condescending treatment she'd received from Zhang Wei every time they'd talked or met.

Wu Chiang was open, caring and highly efficient. Since joining SHH, productivity had increased by over 30% even with the reduced work hours and paid vacation time for all the staff.

Wu walked the two through the entire facility and introduced them to dozens of workers. Holly asked each one if they were enjoying their work. Wu translated for each one. The answer, universally, was yes.

After touring the main storage depot, it was obvious by the way that he was fidgeting that Wu was dying to ask them a question.

"What is it, Mr Chiang?" Holly asked.

"We are one of many distribution and logistics centres for Santa's Helping Hand," Wu began. "Except for one month every year, we distribute emergency supplies to those in need anywhere in our region."

"That's correct," Holly said, nodding.

"Our warehouses are always full," Wu said. "If we have a run on particular items, they are immediately replaced, yet SHH is a registered charity."

"I feel that you have a question," Holly prompted him. "Go ahead. Ask it."

"How is it possible, in these days of financial strain across the planet that this one charitable organisation never has to beg for money or source substandard stock?"

"That's a very good question," Holly said, smiling. "The fact is that we only have one benefactor and he and his wife have very deep pockets and very big hearts."

"But who are they that can afford to spend billions every year just helping those in trouble?" Wu asked.

"I can't say who they are, but I will tell you that they are both very reclusive and very generous."

"May I ask where they live?"

Holly gave him a big smile.

"You won't have heard of the place," Holly said. "It's so far away, it might as well be in a completely different dimension."